I0591495

MINE

Sami A. Abrams

Heart-Stopping Fiction

Copyright © [2025] by [Sami A. Abrams]

All rights reserved.

No portion of this book may be reproduced in any form without written permission from the publisher or author, except as permitted by U.S. copyright law.

This book is fiction. Names, characters, and incidents are the product of the author's imagination or used fictionally. Any resemblance to any actual person, living or dead, events, or locations are entirely coincidental.

contents

ALSO BY Sami

Stone Creek Ranch

Christmas Rodeo Killer

Deadly Rodeo Threat

Rodeo Witness Protector

Dedication

This story is dedicated to the men and women on the Internet Crimes Against Children Task Forces across the country. Your willingness and sacrifice does not go unnoticed. A special thanks to the Sacramento division. You all are amazing!

CHAPTER 1

Wednesday 3:00 p.m.

Another day dealing with the slime of the world. Detective David Whitman sighed and peered out the windshield of the sheriff's department vehicle through his aviators at the ratty house a block ahead. He rolled his neck. Relief accompanied a series of pops.

"Tense much?" His partner and friend Brandon Pierce smacked the piece of gum he'd shoved in his mouth a few minutes ago. A pre-raid habit. One that annoyed David, but if it kept his partner calm, he wouldn't complain. The key to going home after each shift—never lose focus.

He glared at his partner. "Just because you think you're bulletproof doesn't mean I do." He knew all too well how one stray bullet changed lives. He'd lived it.

Get out of your head, man.

David shifted in the passenger seat and adjusted his Kevlar vest. A check of his tactical pants pockets confirmed the extra ammo.

Search warrant Wednesdays. David inhaled, held it for ten seconds, and exhaled. As a member of ICAC—the Internet Crimes Against Children Task Force—he prepped and planned for days like today. Still, he itched with uncertainty. Things could go wrong in an instant. And he refused to lose anyone else he loved. His team, above everything else, was family.

He tapped twice on his vest pocket that held a picture of his parents and sister, plus another of his deceased fiancée. The ritual grounded him during the more dangerous aspect of his job.

"You think he'll be there?" Brandon tapped the steering wheel with his thumbs.

David examined the neighborhood. "Our Confidential Informant had eyes on him a little while ago." He'd repressed the urge to hug his CI when the man disclosed the location of Jimmy Roberts.

One by one, the ICAC team removed child predators from the streets. At times, it seemed the unsavory individuals popped up faster than baby rabbits. But each arrest gave the team a sense of satisfaction that kept them going.

David drummed his fingers on his thigh. The warm summer air draped over him and sweat trickled between his shoulder blades.

"Let's go make friends." Brandon gave him a cheesy grin and slipped from the vehicle.

"Finally." David sent up a quick prayer and followed his partner's actions. His body hummed with adrenaline as he approached the weather-worn cottage.

He and Brandon slipped to either side of the tattered screen at the front entry and placed their backs against the house. He shifted and peeked inside. His line of sight, a direct path through the interior.

Jimmy Roberts, child predator and all-around creep, sprinted toward the rear of the dwelling.

The back door swung open and slammed against the rattrap of a house.

"Pierce!" David flung open the screen door.

"On it!" Brandon's voice trailed off as he jumped from the porch and tore around the side yard. For a guy who had ten years on David, the man could run.

David weaved through the garbage-laden house to the rear exit. The stench made his eyes water. He blinked, clearing his vision, and bolted down the steps into the cluttered backyard.

The suspect had panicked and taken off before David's teammates Sandy and Rick moved to cover the rear entrance.

So much for serving a quiet little warrant.

Beer cans and garbage cluttered the ground making the obstacle course more difficult. He dodged a grill and bumped into a lawn chair. With a grunt, he got his footing and continued the chase.

What happened to Brandon?

"Police! Stop!" David tapped his mic. "Heading north towards the back alley."

"Copy." Sandy's voice wobbled over the radio.

Times like today, he agreed with the people who considered him weird for his choice of work, but he found purpose and maybe a little justice working to take down those who committed crimes against children. Plus, it took him away from the big city streets. After the tragic death of his fiancée, he wanted nothing to do with that world. His heart couldn't take another loss like that.

He vaulted over a small wall. "Police! Stop!" He mentally rolled his eyes. As if that had worked the first time.

Boots crunching in the dried grass, David's foot landed in a shallow hole. His ankle twisted and he stumbled. Fire shot through his leg, but he gritted his teeth and kept running.

The suspect scaled the chain-link fence at the end of the block, flung himself over, and landed at an awkward angle.

David grabbed the top of the metal barrier and swung his leg up, aiming to brace himself with his boot, but missed. His bicep contacted the sharp edge, tearing a ragged path through his skin.

Rolling over the fence, he staggered to his feet, and shoved his knee in Jimmy's back.

"My leg's broken." The man struggled against David's weight.

He fought to slow his racing pulse. "Don't move." Reaching for his zip ties, the sensation of a hot poker stabbing him exploded through his limb. He sucked in a quick breath and glanced at the warm liquid streaming down his arm.

Not what he wanted to deal with today. He had an important appointment tomorrow and refused to miss it for any reason. Including injury.

Unable to procure the restraints, he maintained his position and waited for his teammates.

Brandon rounded the corner and came to an abrupt halt. He handed him a set of handcuffs. "Here."

David secured the suspect and straightened. His adrenaline faded, and light-headedness threatened to knock him over. "Thanks, man. What took you so long?"

"Stupid dog," Brandon muttered and held Jimmy in place.

Thankful for his partner's presence, David slid to the side, fell on his rump, and allowed Brandon to take charge.

David hung his head and gripped his arm to staunch the flow of blood.

Voices mingled in a chaotic buzz as blue and red lights whirled in the distance.

He lifted his chin and caught a glimpse of the paramedics rolling a gurney in his direction. The shrubs and metal fence along the medics' path merged in his vision, then cleared. The haze threatened to take over again. He sucked in air, praying the tunnel disappeared.

He glanced at Jimmy. The man had broken his leg but hadn't seemed to notice the pain. Oblivious, due to a recent dose of drugs, no doubt, the man continued to give Brandon fits.

"What'd you take, Jimmy?" His partner struggled to hold Jimmy on the ground.

"I don't know what you're talking about." Jimmy jerked against Brandon's hold.

Sandy and Rick jogged over.

"Sandy, check the house. Rick, check his pockets." Brandon threw out commands.

"I'm on it." Sandy tossed David a bandana and took off.

Rick crouched next to the suspect. "All right, Jimmy. Anything in your pockets that'll hurt me?"

David's shoulders sagged. His team had things under control.

Grip on the nasty cut, blood trickled between his fingers. His body begged him to go home and catch some shuteye, but the evening was far from over. Part of his team would continue with the search warrant while he and his partner escorted the idiot who'd run to the hospital. Probably not a bad idea since David probably required stitches. He wrapped the bandana around his bicep and pulled it tight with his teeth.

He grumbled and rose to his feet. Swaying, he scrambled to prop himself against the chain-link fence, giving himself a minute to catch his breath and regain his equilibrium.

Definitely not the way he wanted his day to end.

***

"Ambulance, coming in hot."

"Oh, for the love of mud—you're ridiculous." ER nurse Jennie Nielson shook her head as Randy scurried by on his way to prep bays one and two. The young man was a great medical assistant, but the twenty-one-year-old's sense of humor killed her.

She dashed to the entrance, unsure what she'd find.

The Pinewood Shores Emergency Department doors whooshed open, and the warm night air rushed in. Paramedics pushed a gurney through the doublewide entry.

An injured man thrashed on the slim white mattress, and two officers strode beside him. One with a limp.

The small crowd struggled to hold the man in place.

"I'm losing my grip!"

"Don't let go of his good leg!"

Heavy breathing, mixed with grunts, filled the otherwise quiet ER.

Jennie hurried to assist the salt and pepper haired medic she'd grown to love like a father. "What's he on, Mitch?"

"Flakka. What else?"

They whipped the rolling bed into the closest curtain-lined room and set the brakes.

She stood over the agitated man and trapped one of his wrists to the bed.

He kicked out and connected with a metal tray, sending instruments clanking on the floor.

"I've got him." An officer nudged her aside.

She glared at the man next to her. Did she look like she couldn't handle herself? Sure, he had four or five inches on her five-seven frame and probably outweighed her by seventy-five pounds, but really? She had a job to do, and he'd butted in.

Doctor Jeremy Bennett scurried into the bay with Jennie's nurse friend Tammy on his heels. Tammy tightened the straps across the patient's body and added her weight to restrain the injured man.

"Nielson, take care of Detective Whitman. It seems trouble found him again." Bennett raised a brow at the officer.

The detective's partner took over, and Whitman wrapped his hand around his bicep.

"Yes, doctor." Her gaze landed on the officer's upper arm. Blood had soaked the cloth wrapped around his arm. "Sir, if you'll follow me."

The detective grumbled. He limped to the next bay and slid onto the exam table.

Jennie grabbed the white cloth screen.

"Leave it open."

She pivoted. "Excuse me?"

"Don't shut the curtain." His tone left no room for argument.

Just what she needed, another overbearing, controlling, egotistical man—Not. Of course, she might be a little jaded after barely surviving her living nightmare. "Listen, Detective—"

"David."

She bit the inside of her cheek, keeping the sarcasm from tumbling from her lips. Law enforcement officers had a reputation for having a take-charge demeanor, and rightly so, but this man tried her patience.

Let it go and do your job.

She inhaled and returned her attention to the supply tray. "Okay—*David*. What happened?" Jennie snapped on a clean pair of blue latex gloves and turned to face him.

He jutted his chin toward the man that continued to struggle against those trying to treat him. "Bad guy over there decided to run. I twisted my ankle and sliced my arm on the edge of a metal fence."

She unwrapped the bandana around David's arm. The jagged gash required stitches, but not severe enough for immediate attention. She rinsed the wound with saline and rewrapped his bicep with a compression wrap until the doctor had time to stitch the cut, then moved to his ankle and poked and prodded.

He hissed in a breath.

"Well, tough guy, the good news, neither are too serious. Bad news, you'll be sore, and you'll need a few stitches. Plus, a tetanus shot if you're not up to date." She could have sworn the man turned green. "Something wrong?"

The muscles in his jaw twitched. "Just hate needles."

"Good to know." She pursed her lips to hide the grin pulling at her lips. Served Mr. Takeover-My-Job right for sticking his nose where he didn't belong.

He narrowed his gaze. "You look like you're having a little too much fun with that piece of info."

She sighed and mentally reprimanded herself. "Sorry. That wasn't nice of me. I promise to be gentle."

David studied her, then nodded. "I appreciate that."

A grunt and crash caught Jennie off guard. The suspect broke through the restraint, grabbed a pair of scissors, and drew his arm back. She stood paralyzed. Her gaze shifted to Detective Whitman.

David's eyes widened. He flew off the hospital bed and tackled her. His forearm smacked across her face.

The scissors clanged against the wall and tumbled to the floor.

"Stay down," he growled in her ear.

Her cheek throbbed, and her pulse raced. "Get off me!"

She clawed and fought to get away. Crawling to the opposite wall, she hugged her knees.

The heat of her swollen face and the sensation of a man pinning her down had her heart fighting to pound out of her ribcage.

Shoes scuffled on the floor and shouts echoed in the small area.

Jennie froze. She had to assist, but her body refused to cooperate. Her mind tumbled to the past. Her ex-boyfriend Kenny's fist contacting her face and hateful words spewing from his lips.

"Jennie." A voice flittered through the haze. "Nielson!" Doctor Bennett's command snapped her back to the present.

She scrambled to her feet. "Yes, sir."

"10 milligrams Diazepam. Now!" Bennett strained to push the patient's shoulders to the bed while Mitch, both officers, and Tammy each grabbed a limb.

She hurried to get the medication and fumbled with the syringe. Inhaling, she clutched the man's forearm and inserted the sedative into his upper arm. She added her weight to Tammy's and held tight until the medication took effect.

Doctor Bennett released his hold. "Well, that was fun, boys and girls."

Taking two steps backward, she absorbed the sight. Everyone appeared frazzled. The man had ripped the IV from his arm. Blood splattered the white sheets and the floor—not to mention her own scrubs and the detective's polo shirt. A massacre scene from a horror movie came to mind.

Blood flowed down David's arm.

Her gaze locked with his. Color washed from his face.

"Detective, I think you better sit down." She clasped his uninjured arm and led him to the adjacent bed.

He dropped his chin to his chest. "I don't feel...."

"Mitch!"

The paramedic scrambled to her side. He grabbed the officer under the arms, and she lifted the man's legs. Together, they swung the detective onto the mattress.

She unwrapped the bandage. The fight had caused the wound to split further, and his arm bled at an alarming rate from the physical stress.

She applied pressure to his cut to stem the bleeding. "Doc, I need you as soon as you're free." Taking a deep breath, she willed her stomach to uncoil, but the swelling on her cheekbone made it impossible to shake the internal fear.

David's eyes fluttered open. His unfocused gaze landed on her. He blinked.

"Welcome back." Jennie grabbed supplies with her free hand. She cleaned and prepped the detective's arm. "Doctor Bennett will be here in a minute to stitch you back together."

"Thanks." He touched his forehead. "Can't believe I passed out."

"It happens." She shrugged and continued her care.

He grabbed her wrist. "Listen. I want to...."

The panic alarm inside her head went off. She jerked from his grip. "Don't!"

CHAPTER 2

Wednesday 11:00 p.m.

Hands tight on the steering wheel, Jennie aimed her sedan toward home. Her face flamed hot at the memory of her reaction during her shift. She'd made a fool of herself in front of the handsome detective. After Kenny had come close to ending her life, she'd escaped under the radar to her Aunt Emily's in Pinewood Shores. She'd settled in and loved the small-town life, but now she wanted to hide in a hole and never come out.

Please don't ever make me cross paths with Detective Whitman again.

Streetlights glowed, creating shadows along the sidewalks. Jennie's shoulders tensed as she maneuvered the car through town. She hated the dark. Evil hid in the corners, waiting to jump out, or so her mind told her. Especially tonight.

What had been a calm day had turned into a nightmare. One that her brain refused to release. The recollection of her near-death experience at the hands of Kenny flashbacked in full color when Detective Whitman attempted to help her. His hands on her triggered the memory of the worst day of her life.

When would her past quit haunting her?

She'd conceived her precocious ten-year-old daughter Zoey in her rush to find love. The bad choices in Jennie's life stacked higher than the tallest building in the city, but she'd never include Zoey in that list. Her heart belonged to that young girl. Young and stupid, Jennie had walked away from her college friends and Aunt Emily for a future with Brad. It hadn't taken long for her to realize she'd married a drunk. He'd loved her in his own sad way and had given her Zoey. For that, she'd forever be grateful. But after his death, her decisions had gotten worse.

Jennie turned into her driveway and shut off the engine. The porch light illuminated the front door and chased away darkness on the path. She inhaled, staring at the short walk.

Her heart raced. She struggled to grab the truth. Kenny had four more years on his ten-year prison sentence and wasn't outside watching—waiting to finish what he'd started.

Hand in her purse, she wrapped her fingers around her stun gun and sprinted inside. She slammed the door closed and flipped the three strong locks. A little overkill, but her Aunt Emily, who owned the cottage, hadn't blinked when Jennie requested the extra security measure.

She rested her back against the wall and fought the tears flooding her eyes. Her cheek throbbed where Detective Whitman had taken her to the ground to protect her from the crazed patient. Then she'd tumbled into a flashback and embarrassed herself. She hadn't had a reaction like tonight's in over a year and hated the regression to the dark places of her past.

Breathe deep. You can do it. She talked herself through the swarming panic and willed her pulse to slow.

Her trembling fingers hit speed dial. One ring. Two rings. A tear slipped down Jennie's cheek. Three rings. *Come on, Tina, pick up.*

"Hello."

"Tina." Her voice quivered.

"Jennie, what's wrong?"

"Tonight...Panicked...He thinks...freak." Her inability to get the words out only made the sobs come harder.

"Slow down, honey. Okay. Let me get this straight. Something happened, and you panicked."

"Uh-huh." She sucked in a breath, trying to gain control.

"And someone thinks you're a freak?"

"Uh-huh."

"You'll have to give me more to go on than that, my friend."

Jennie took a deep breath, then another. "Sorry."

"Better?"

"A bit." Just hearing Tina's calm tone helped.

"Want to try that again?"

Jennie laughed. "I'm surprised you got as much as you did." She sniffed then proceeded to explain what had happened in the emergency room.

"Oh, honey. I'm sure he doesn't think that. And if he did, he's not worth your energy."

"It was humiliating. I have no idea what my coworkers think about me now. And the detective...." She covered her face with her hands.

"Next time you go to work, hold your head high. You're an awesome nurse. Don't forget that. And if that detective so much as says one negative thing about you, tell him he'll face my wrath."

Jennie smiled. "Thanks, Tina." She wiped tears from her cheeks. Her chest loosened and she took her first full deep breath since she arrived home.

"Anytime, honey."

"I miss you."

"Ah, girl, I miss you too. Maybe someday soon, I'll come visit."

Except for her once-a-year visit, Tina had stayed away to guard Jennie's location. She appreciated her protectiveness. But Jennie didn't have many friends. "Promise?"

"You know it. Feel better?"

"Yes. Thanks for listening."

"Any time, my friend."

They said their goodbyes.

Jennie pushed to a stand. Once her legs quit wobbling, she moved to her bedroom. The phone call with Tina helped, but the deep-seated fear lingered in the quiet house.

After changing clothes, she crawled under the fluffy light green duvet that wrapped her in a false sense of security. She felt like a child hiding under blankets from imaginary monsters. But her monster had proven real and had almost cost her her life. She glanced at her bedside lamp but couldn't convince herself to turn it off.

Thankfully, Zoey had stayed the night with Aunt Emily and hadn't witnessed Jennie's panic attack. She'd never kept the truth from Zoey, and the young girl knew more than anyone her age ever should. She refused to allow her daughter to endure the same horrors again.

The thought of Kenny made Jennie's nerves zing like live wires. She snatched her cell phone from the nightstand and clasped it to her chest like her life depended on it.

Because if Kenny got out of prison, the phone might be the only thing that saved her life.

**

Thursday 7:00 a.m.

David hobbled to the living room with the phone to his ear, listening to his mom chatter on about him getting hurt, and halted in front of the family pictures that lined the fireplace mantel. He stepped closer and studied the photo of his parents and his sister. He struggled to pull air into his lungs when his gaze landed on Brenda. His fiancée had died three years ago from a gunshot wound. The ache refused to dissipate. The woman he'd longed to spend the rest of his life with—gone.

"David?"

"Sorry, Mom. Got lost in thought looking at family pictures."

"She loved you, you know."

A lump occupied his throat. He nodded even though she couldn't see him. "I know."

"You could take it down if it's too hard."

He swallowed hard and traced the frame with his finger. "No. I don't want to forget her."

"I know it hurts, but she wouldn't want you to go through life alone."

He snorted. "Subtle, Mom."

She laughed. "Would I love to see you married and give me grandkids? Yes. But more than anything, I want to see you happy."

"Thanks."

A horn honked outside.

"I better go before my partner wakes the neighborhood."

"Go. But please be careful."

"I will, Mom. Bye." David tucked the phone into his pocket and closed the front door behind him.

Brandon waved from his department-issued vehicle. David inhaled the morning air as he hobbled to the passenger side and collapsed in the seat.

"How'd it go?"

"Better than I expected. Mom didn't give me too much grief."

His partner laughed and pulled away from the house for the short drive to the school.

Tall pines dotted the street outside Pinewood Shores Elementary. Deciduous trees intermixed with the evergreens had splotches of yellow and orange—a sign that fall was coming, even though the heat continued to linger.

He loved the small town. He hated the reason for the change in location, but aside from the loss of his fiancée, he'd made a good choice to make Pinewood Shores his new home.

He strode to the school entrance and held the door open for his partner. They checked in with the front office and chatted with the administrative assistant. He attached the visitor badge to his shirt and headed to room eight.

The main hallway brought back memories of his own elementary school. Some of his fondest recollections were from his second-grade class. His teacher that year made him feel special.

Boots clacking on the hard floors, he and Brandon continued down the hall.

His partner's sister taught fifth grade and had requested their annual presentation on cell phone and internet safety. He'd come with Brandon to Meredith's classroom several times since he'd transferred to Pinewood Shores three years ago.

Brandon pushed the classroom door open and waltzed in. A big grin graced his partner's face when his gaze landed on his sister.

David sniffed and wrinkled his nose. The stench of sweat and body odor made his eyes water. *Mental note to self, put Vapor Rub under your nose next time you visit a fifth-grade class.* He gave Meredith a quick hug and faced the ten and eleven-year-old crowd.

After introductions, he and Brandon went into their speech about not trusting strangers on social media and only communicating with people they knew.

Glancing around the room at thirty faces, he spotted one young girl whose attention had never wavered. Most of the students either rolled their eyes or chose to stare off into space, but not the girl in a light green t-shirt with a rainbow-colored unicorn declaring, *I believe in unicorns.*

Good for her. Maybe the girl had listened, and his words hadn't gone unheard.

He had to at least try to crack *the nothing can happen to me* shell of these kids. They'd seen too many young boys and girls caught up in the social media world talking to the wrong people and end up victims of the slime bags who lured them in.

"If anyone has any questions or would like a business card, please come see me on your way out." David glanced at the clock. Right on time.

Merideth stepped forward. "Okay, kids, time for recess. Please be sure to thank Detectives Whitman and Pierce. See you in a little while."

Thank yous pinged around the room as students gathered their snacks and left the classroom.

Several stopped for cards, but most rushed out the door chattering about what they intended to play once they finished eating.

A girl who'd listened attentively stopped in front of him. Gazing up, she tilted her head. "You're serious about the dangers, aren't you?"

David crouched to eye level. "I am. Please be careful. I'd hate to see anything happen to you."

Her brow scrunched. He could see the wheels turning.

She held out her palm. "May I please have a card?"

"Sure thing." He placed it in her hand. "What's your name?"

"Zoey."

Beautiful blue eyes stared at him. "Never hesitate to call if something doesn't feel right."

The young girl bit her lip. She finally nodded, slipped the card into her back pocket, and walked out of sight.

David sighed. He hoped more of the students had listened. His stomach twisted at the thought of any of them lured into the trap of some sick and twisted creep.

His partner's hand landed on his shoulder. "Relax, man. We can only give young people the information. The rest is in God's hands."

"Right." Maybe a few years ago, he'd have trusted God. After his mistakes that had cost him everything, he wasn't sure God valued the same things he did.

***

Thursday 6:00 p.m.

Each slice of the onion stung, causing tears to well. Jennie squeezed her eyes shut, hoping for relief from the offending food. She wiped the back of her wrist across her cheek, careful not to put pressure on her bruise, and hurried to complete the task. If her daughter didn't love extra onions in her chili, she wouldn't be in the kitchen looking like she'd lost her best friend.

"Mom?" Zoey yelled from the other room.

"Yeah, honey?" Jennie scraped the onions into the pot of meat and beans sitting on the stove, then rushed to the sink. She scrubbed her hands with soap and rinsed her eyes with water.

Her daughter burst into the room. "Look at what Aunt Emily bought me."

Eyes closed, Jennie patted the counter and located the towel. Blotting her face dry, she pivoted and found Zoey spinning in a circle. The light green dress with coral and white flowers flared at the bottom.

"It's beautiful. You look so grown up." Jennie pushed the hair from her forehead with the back of her hand. She sighed. Where had her baby gone? Only a few more years until her little girl became a teenager. Time moved too fast.

"I want to send a selfie to Aunt Tina." Zoey posed and snapped the picture with her new cell phone, one Jennie had purchased last week to stay in contact with her daughter.

Jennie's heart ached at the thought of Tina, her best friend from Indiana. When she'd escaped her ex-boyfriend's abuse, and the police put him behind bars for attempting to kill her, she'd broken all ties to that life. Except one. Tina.

"Sure. Go ahead." She rattled off her friend's number. "Why don't you add her to your contact list while you're at it."

"Yes!" Zoey's fingers flew over the keypad, paused, and then typed more.

A smile curved on Jennie's lips. Tina must have enjoyed the contact with Zoey if the flying text messages were any indication.

Her daughter placed her phone on the counter and lifted the lid to the chili pot. Inhaling, she grinned. "Thanks for making my favorite dinner."

Ruffling her daughter's hair, she chuckled. "You know I love you if I'm willing to chop onions."

Giggles erupted from her mini-me. The only difference between them was Zoey's darker hair. The same color as her father Brad's. A stab of pain clutched her chest. Her deceased husband had been far from perfect, but she had loved him all the same.

The cell phone pinged.

Zoey snatched the device and swiped open the text message. Her blue eyes widened, and a whimper escaped.

Jennie grabbed the phone and read the message.

You're such a beautiful young lady. Do you have any more pictures?

A lump formed in Jennie's throat. "Who did you send this to?"

"I-I thought I was chatting with Aunt Tina."

"Well, it's definitely not her." Jennie's voice cracked. Some stranger had a picture of her baby girl.

"I'm sorry, momma." Zoey's lips quivered.

"I know you didn't mean to." She checked the number. Zoey had transposed two of the digits of the area code. Jennie's fingers hovered over the keypad. "I'm going to give this guy a piece of my mind."

Zoey gripped Jennie's wrist, halting her from typing. "No, momma. Wait. Don't do that."

"Why on Earth not?" In her opinion, the sooner someone told the man off, the better.

"Because..." Zoey ran to her room and returned with a card. "Let me call the detective."

"What detective?" How had her daughter gotten her hands on a police officer's business card?

Petite hands waved the small paper. "Two detectives came to our school today. They told us to call if anything weird ever happened." Zoey took the phone, punched in the number, and held it to her ear. "Detective? This is Zoey from school. I have a problem."

CHAPTER 3

Thursday 7:00 p.m.

Under normal circumstances, David preferred driving. His partner drove like a ninety-nine-year-old grandmother. But after last night's incident and subsequent stitches and fainting episode, Brandon refused to trust him behind the wheel. David had pointed out that he'd made it home without incident earlier, but Brandon only shook his head and told him to stop complaining. He was currently at the man's mercy.

David's mind raced as fast as the trees whizzing by. Only this morning, he'd handed Zoey his number, and the young girl had already called. "I wonder what happened over the past several hours?"

"I have no idea, but at least we know she listened."

"That's true. I guess we'll find out in a few minutes."

His partner grunted his response.

David exhaled and stared at the passing scenery. His mind drifted to the nurse who'd witnessed his embarrassing fainting spell last night. Her reaction when he tried to help her made his skin crawl. He'd witnessed too much violence in his career not to notice the aftereffects of abuse when he saw it. He debated whether to do some digging on her behalf or let it be. Right. He wasn't the *let it be* type of guy.

"This is it." Brandon's comment pulled him from his thoughts.

His partner parked at the curb in front of a bright yellow bungalow with cedar steps leading to a white porch. Planter boxes hung from the rail, red and pink geraniums spilling over the edge. A matching white picket fence enclosed the property.

"Looks like a quaint little cottage." David swung open the passenger door and stepped onto the sidewalk.

"If I recall, this is Emily Hanover's place." Brandon joined him.

He glanced at his partner. "I thought she lived in town." Pinewood Shores was a small enough town that he knew most folks on sight but big enough he could still keep a few secrets. He didn't want his failure known all over town.

"She does. She inherited the property years ago and turned it into a rental sometime in the past six or so years."

No wonder he hadn't known. He'd only recently moved to Pinewood Shores and hadn't learned all the details of the town's residents—yet.

David strode up the steps and knocked on the door.

The wooden door swung open, and Zoey's face pressed against the screen.

"Detective. You came." The girl's face flashed with relief. She called over her shoulder. "Momma, the detectives are here." The outer door flung open.

He and Brandon entered the comfortable looking cottage.

A beautiful blonde waltzed in, hair in a messy bun, wiping her hands on a towel. "Sorry. I'm in the middle of...." She froze. Her eyes widened. "Detective Whitman?"

Great. Just what he needed. Jennie Nielson, the nurse who'd witnessed his embarrassing emergency room blackout. "Ma'am."

"What are you doing here?"

"This young lady called." He gestured to Zoey. "Said she needed help. I'm assuming she's your daughter."

Jennie sighed. "Right." Her gaze landed on his partner. "Sorry for my lack of manners. I don't think we were formally introduced yesterday at the hospital. I'm Jennie Nielson, and this is my daughter, Zoey."

"Brandon Pierce. Nice to meet you, ladies." Brandon shook their hands.

Zoey's gaze darted between her mom and David. "You two know each other?"

He started to answer, but Jennie piped in before he could respond. "I met Detective Whitman at the hospital last night." She rested her hands on Zoey's shoulders. "Why don't you gentlemen come on in and have a seat. Since my daughter contacted you, I'll let her explain."

The young girl straightened, and David could have sworn she glowed with pride.

He and Brandon sat on either end of the tan couch while Jennie took the navy-blue easy chair off to the side. Removing the floral pillow from behind her, Jennie hugged it to her chest.

Zoey propped herself on the armrest next to her mom and filled them in on the text message gone wrong. "So, you see. I thought I was talking with Aunt Tina. But it wasn't her. Mom says I got two numbers mixed up."

Tapping his pencil on the notebook he'd used to record the information, David set his jaw. The girl's story made sense. One simple transposition of numbers. An unfortunate mistake that had dire consequences.

"Thanks, Zoey." He lifted his gaze to Jennie. Tension snaked across her features, causing him to pause. Her response last night spoke of a brutal past. Had today's incident been fallout from that? Or had he read her reaction wrong?

He hated to ask the woman, but he had to cover all the possibilities. "Is there anyone who'd want to scare or hurt you or your daughter?"

Zoey jerked. Her wide blue eyes focused on her mother.

A protective hand rested on the girl's back. Jennie cleared her throat. "Detective, with all due respect, this was purely a misdial. Nothing more."

The evasion of his question hadn't gone unnoticed. The woman hid something. "Please understand that I have to do my job and ask the hard questions."

She nodded.

"I'm curious why Zoey didn't have her aunt's number programmed into her phone."

Jennie's shoulders relaxed. "Tina's not technically her aunt, and I purchased the phone a week ago. It only has my number, her great aunt's number, and a couple of approved friends. I bought it so she could get a hold of me if needed. I'm a single parent. I don't have backup."

Brandon leaned forward and rested his forearms on his knees. "May I ask where her father is?"

Relieved his partner took that question, David settled back against the couch.

"Her father died before she was born." Jennie gritted her teeth. "Drunk driving accident."

Brandon's voice softened. "Sorry to hear that, ma'am. Was the driver convicted?"

The woman threaded her fingers through her daughter's hair and sighed. "My late husband *was* the drunk."

David glanced at Brandon and returned his attention to the two ladies in front of him.

Time to rescue his partner. David cleared his throat. "How about social media? Anyone bothering you online, Zoey?"

The young girl shook her head. "I don't have any accounts, and neither does my mom."

No social media? Law enforcement officers tended to stay away from those sites but to have nothing... "Really? That's unusual for today's world."

"We like our privacy, detective. Is there anything else? I need to feed Zoey and get her ready for bed. Tomorrow's a school day."

David had struck a nerve with his question, which increased his curiosity. What had happened to this woman? He slapped his knees and stood. His partner followed his lead. "I have nothing more for now, but I'd like to take Zoey's phone to figure out who this guy is."

Jennie nodded at her daughter, and Zoey headed to the kitchen. When she returned, she held out the device to David.

He lowered himself to eye level with the fifth grader. "I'll get this back to you as soon as possible."

"Thank you." Zoey smiled.

The lack of protest from the girl puzzled him. Most preteens would have thrown a fit about losing their phones.

"I appreciate you coming by." Jennie led them to the front door.

He hadn't noticed the three heavy-duty locks when they'd arrived. His mind spun, attempting to put the clues about this woman together.

Halting his thoughts to examine later, he stepped onto the front porch. "Not a problem. That's what we're here for. I'll let you know if we find anything and get the phone back to Zoey as soon as possible."

"She might not have many contacts on it, but she doesn't like to be without it." Jennie chewed on her lower lip. "*I* don't like her to be without it."

He nodded his understanding. What young person didn't want their phone with them at all times? That took him back to his lack of protest observation from earlier. "Goodnight, ma'am."

"Goodnight, detectives."

The door clicked shut behind him. He took a moment to allow his eyes to adjust. The dusk of evening on their arrival had turned into the black of night.

He meandered down the dimly lit pathway, trailing Brandon to the car. Once buckled in, he turned to his partner. "Well?"

"I think it's just like it sounds, and we're fortunate that at least one of my sister's students listened." Brandon hesitated.

"But?"

His partner shrugged.

"Oh no, you don't. You're not clamming up on me. You think Jennie and Zoey are hiding from someone, don't you?"

Brandon flipped on the headlights and pulled from the curb. "Affirmative. We're on the same page, partner."

David scratched the back of his neck and scanned the street out of habit. "I don't want to pry into their personal lives, but what if this isn't random?"

"I'm hearing you loud and clear." Brandon stopped at the intersection and turned left. "Before we do a full background check, why don't we talk to Emily Hanover? Maybe she can give us some insight into her tenant."

"Sounds like a plan."

David's gut twisted. In his line of work, he saw terrible things happen to people all the time. He had a bad feeling and was unsure he wanted to know what horrible thing had happened to Jennie.

***

Palm on the door, Jennie had held her breath until she heard the detectives' car drive away. She couldn't afford to have the police pry into her life. Not that they would discover anything criminal, at least not for her. The possibility that the detectives' digging would bring evil to her door—a chance she couldn't afford. Then again, only one person from her old life knew her location, and Tina would die before she told anyone.

"Momma? Did I mess up by calling Detective Whitman?"

Jennie cupped Zoey's face in her hands. "No, baby. I'm glad you called. You did the right thing."

Zoey chewed her bottom lip. "But what if they—"

"No." She kissed the top of her daughter's head. "We've been safe for six years. Maybe it's time to quit hiding and start living."

Zoey grinned. "I can't believe you said that."

"Neither can I." She chuckled. "You've never complained, and I admire you for that. But I think it's time you have a normal childhood. No ten-year-old should be forced to be anonymous."

Small arms wrapped around Jennie's waist. "I love you, Momma."

"Please be cautious. Even normal kids can't be careless."

"I know. I'm not stupid." Zoey rolled her eyes.

Jennie shook her head. The teenage years zoomed at her like a racecar. "Go eat and get ready for bed." She spun her daughter to face the kitchen and gave her a pat on the backside.

Zoey skipped away, her brown hair bouncing with each step.

She massaged her temples. Protecting her daughter had consumed her life for the past six years, and in a single moment, the security net she'd had in place since she moved to Pinewood Shores disintegrated with a simple reversal of a couple of numbers.

Had the safe haven of Aunt Emily's cottage disappeared? She took in the personal touches she'd added to her home. The picture above the small fireplace she and Zoey had picked out their first year in town. The couch and easy chair she'd bought with her first paycheck as a nurse. Tears welled as the truth hit her. A mistaken text and a creep after her daughter had violated her sanctuary.

She flopped onto the sofa and buried her face in her hands.

Would the detectives pry into her life and discover her mistakes?

She'd worked hard to overcome those lapses in judgment. All that effort only to have her past unravel before her eyes. So much for the positive reputation that she'd built in this lakeside community. If anyone found out... Tears pricked and threatened to fall.

Her hand touched her bruised cheekbone. The same one Kenny had shattered and the doctors had reconstructed.

Zoey deserved more than a life of fear—and so did Jennie.

CHAPTER 4

Friday 9:00 a.m.

Curtains drawn in his one-bedroom apartment, he logged onto his preferred websites. A little something to enjoy after a long day's work. The stark living space needed a woman's touch, and he planned to find the one woman who'd make those changes—Jennie Nielson. She'd eluded him for years, but he'd find her. Until then, he'd enjoy his favorite pastime.

Image after image flashed across his computer screen. Each young girl as pretty as the next. He jolted to a stop from scanning the photos.

Zoey?

He leaned forward and studied the photo. He'd never mistake those blue eyes. He smiled at his discovery. Zoey had grown into a beautiful young lady. Just like her momma.

"Well, well, what do you know. Not as smart as you think, are you, Jennie? I knew you couldn't hide forever." His multiyear search had ended, thanks to his *hobby*. He'd found a link to *his* woman.

After her release from the hospital, she'd vanished. He'd had eyes on her until he didn't. The nurse had helped Jennie into a white sedan, and then poof, she'd disappeared along with Zoey. His jaw clenched. The ungrateful wench. This time he'd make sure she understood who she belonged to.

He worked on tracing the origin of the picture and hit wall after wall. Unsavory words spewed from his mouth. He had the skill set, but these jerks had covered their tracks. He would find Jennie and make her life miserable for running from him.

Three hours later, he sat back, a grin spread across his face. "Gotcha."

Plans took shape in his head. He'd torment her until fear got the best of her. Then he'd make his move and take back what was his.

He envisioned the terror on Jennie's pretty face when she realized he'd come for her. He laughed and grabbed his keys. "No one else can have you, Jennie. You're mine."

***

Friday 1:00 p.m.

Cup of coffee in hand, David slouched in a conference room office chair, reminding himself why he'd joined the ICAC task force. The grim reality of the work tore at his heart most days. That's why he and Brandon had decorated the two-person cubicle at the Landon County Sheriff's Department office with stupid comic strips and ridiculous signs to combat the weight of the job. Some days he wished he could scrub out his brain and erase all the horrors he'd witnessed. But saving children from predators gave him purpose. And relieved a smidge of guilt from his fiancée's death.

He closed his eyes and inhaled the rising steam, allowing the bold aroma to penetrate his sleep-deprived brain. An IV infusion of caffeine might give him the jolt he needed, but he doubted it.

Wednesday night, while David and Brandon had dealt with the suspect, the lab techs had recovered evidence from the search warrant. The physical items twisted his stomach in knots, but the cyber data made him want to vomit. A link to a website on Jimmy Roberts's computer screamed child predator and caught the attention of their resident tech guru Megan. Yesterday David had signed over the evidence into her capable hands. He prayed it led them to more arrests and shut down the scumbags' operation.

After dropping Zoey's cell phone off at the station at eight o'clock last night, he'd headed home. Sleep had eluded him during the brief couple hours he laid in bed. His mind lingered on the creep who'd attempted to lure in the sweet girl he'd met at the elementary school. The thought of her not calling or deciding to continue the conversation with the man added to his soured stomach.

When a call came at midnight requesting a team meeting, he'd stumbled out of bed and dragged himself to the office. The one a.m. start time had his head pounding.

Twelve hours later, papers and laptops covered the conference table. The Internet Crimes Against Children task force had worked non-stop, and fatigue had taken its toll.

Rick leaned back in his chair and closed his eyes twenty minutes ago. His soft snores filled the room.

David's gaze landed on Sandy, who sat opposite him. Her head lay in the crook of her elbow on top of her closed laptop. Her hair stuck out in multiple directions from her usual smooth ponytail.

The team was early in the investigation and already running on fumes.

Megan's voice emanated from the speaker. "Dude. You still there?"

He shook his head, dislodging the preverbal cobwebs. "Yeah. Just barely."

"Well, wake up. Those strange bits of data—I connected them."

"What?" David leaned his chest across the table and brought himself as close as possible to the phone speaker.

Brandon ambled in and ran his hand over his head.

David jerked his head toward the phone and mouthed *Megan.* His partner nodded and fell into a seat beside him.

"You heard me, genius."

"Megs, I'm exhausted. Spell it out for me." He blinked. He needed more caffeine.

"Your Roberts is tied to the website of the ick and famous. He's not the owner but a big contributor."

"How's Zoey's text connected?"

"I matched the picture from her phone to a picture on the website. Not sure who's who in the creep yearbook, but they tie together somehow. I'm guessing Jimmy uploaded her picture for unsavory reasons."

He clenched his fist. "That's just great. Zoey's picture is out there for any child predator to see."

"Sorry, David." Empathy oozed through the line.

Brandon shifted in his seat. "Can you remove the photo?"

"Not a good idea."

David straightened and smacked his hand on the tabletop. "Why not?"

Rick and Sandy startled awake and stared at him.

A heavy sigh over the phone met his ears. "Because we'd tip them off, and they'd shut it down and move on."

"Oh yeah, there is that." David rubbed his gritty eyes. "I just don't like Zoey's picture out there for every disgusting excuse for a human to ogle."

"Then get back to work, find the bad guys, and arrest them." Megan's matter-of-fact tone would have brought a smile to David's face if frustration hadn't taken over.

"We're trying, Megs. Thanks for the help. Let us know if you find anything else."

"Will do." A click, then silence lingered in the room.

Sandy unwrapped the scrunchy from her hair and smoothed out her locks. She gathered the strands and redid her ponytail. "All right, boys. Let's get busy. Brandon—any more coffee out there? Rick—check out the webpage and see if you can turn up anything new. David—you and I will hunt down known associates of Jimmy Roberts."

David raised an eyebrow, glanced at Brandon, then back at Sandy.

She tilted her head and pinched her lips together.

"Why did I get coffee duty?" Brandon huffed.

She rolled her eyes in dramatic fashion. "Because you're the only one who can make it drinkable. Duh."

"True." Brandon chuckled. "I'm on it."

David locked his gaze on her. "And when did you become queen?"

"Since you're too tired to think straight." Sandy's tone softened. The woman wasn't wrong. Brain function was at a premium right now.

The ICAC team dug in and searched the internet and contacted informants for the next couple of hours.

"I'm getting nowhere." David stood and stretched. Pops rippled down his back. His mind drifted to Jennie's avoidance of certain questions last night. He'd intended to visit Emily Hanover today, but the late-night call-in had thrown off his plan.

"Something about Jennie Nielson's story isn't sitting right with me. I'm taking a break and am heading over to chat with Mrs. Hanover. See if she has any information we can use."

With his eyes focused on the laptop screen, Brandon waved. "Cookies would be nice if you can finagle a box."

David laughed. "I'll see what I can do." Ambling from the conference room, he stepped outside and squinted at the bright June sun. He slipped on his sunglasses and soaked in the warmth before sliding into the driver's seat and pulling away from the station.

Several minutes later, David sauntered up the rosebush-lined sidewalk to Emily Hanover's craftsman-style home in downtown Pinewood Shores. Known by the town for her beautiful flower gardens, the older woman loved to share her oasis. She'd created a sitting area in her front yard for public use. Residents stopped by on a daily basis and rested or ate lunch on the wooden benches next to the Koi Pond and three-tiered fountain.

Rumor had it that years after she'd welcomed the good people of the sleepy town to her peaceful retreat, she'd confided in friends that the idea had helped combat the loneliness of losing her husband.

David reflected on his own loss. He understood the desire to fill the emptiness with company. Throwing himself into work and the Wednesday night pick-up basketball games at the local gym with the guys had brought him through his darkest days.

He'd moved to Pinewood Shores and joined the ICAC team three years ago. The members had become family. As draining as the work could be, he relished the successes.

People often asked him why he'd transferred to such a depressing department. What those around him didn't understand, saving children from the clutches of those who wanted to exploit them, gave him a satisfaction homicide never had.

His mind wandered to the determined little girl he'd met yesterday. What would have happened if he hadn't given Zoey his business card?

Standing at the entrance of Miss Emily's house, he pushed the doorbell. Church-like chimes rang in the background.

The ornate oak door creaked open, and a sixty-something lady with gray streaks in her brown hair greeted him.

"Detective Whitman, it's good to see you. Come on in." She motioned to the living room.

A beautiful rock fireplace adorned the far wall. A dark green couch, floral chair, and glass coffee table invited visitors to sit and chat. He'd spent many hours in this room over the past few years, eating cookies like a five-year-old and enjoying the older woman's company. And yet, he didn't know much about her family other than stories of her late husband.

"Thank you, Miss Emily." He made his way to the sofa and lowered himself to the edge of the cushion. Resting his elbows on his knees, he clasped his hands and inhaled.

The scent of baked cookies tickled his nose. Snickerdoodles if he wasn't mistaken. His stomach complained about the lack of lunch today. Once he finished here, he'd swing by the café and grab an early dinner.

Mrs. Hanover relaxed in the easy chair next to him. "What can I do for you, young man? Did you come for a treat, or is there something else on your mind?"

He chuckled at the woman's perceptiveness. "I'm hoping you can give me a bit of information. I met your tenant last night and would like to know a little about her background."

"Oh, really?" The woman grinned.

Great. David hadn't meant it to sound personal. "Not like that."

"Like what?" She quirked an eyebrow.

"Miss Emily. Please. I'm trying to do my job here." He could count on one hand the number of times people hadn't bugged him about his single status. The pleasures of a tight-knit community.

Mrs. Hanover's brow creased. "Why would you need information about Jennie?"

"Jennie and Zoey ran into a bit of trouble last night. Brandon and I went to help, but we have a concern we hope you can clear up."

The woman's jaw twitched, and her gaze landed on her cell phone then shifted back to him. "What happened?"

"I won't go into detail, but Zoey texted a stranger by mistake. I'm covering all my bases to find out who and keep the mother and daughter safe."

"What do you need to know?" Her knuckles whitened as she tightened her grip on the arms of her chair.

His gaze drifted from her hands to her face. "How well do you know your renter?"

A soft smile curved on Emily's lips. "I'd say I know Jennie quite well."

He arched an eyebrow and waited for her to continue, but the woman stared him down like a pro.

Strange. Even Miss Emily seemed to be hiding something.

"Mrs. Hanover..." he grumbled.

"Don't Mrs. Hanover me, young man."

David ducked his head, embarrassed by the scolding from the town's favorite lady. "Sorry, ma'am."

"That's better. Now, to answer your question, Jennie is my niece. She lived with me for a couple of years as a teen after her mother died from an overdose. I loved my sister, but she hadn't always made the smartest choices."

"You raised your niece? Why haven't I ever heard this? I don't think Brandon even knows."

"Probably not. Jennie is a lot younger than Brandon, and she tended to keep to herself. She moved to Indiana twelve years ago with a man who promised her a good life. It didn't take long for her to realize she'd married an alcoholic. But I'll give him this, he treated her well. She loved him and was committed to their marriage, so she stayed." The older woman tsked. "Then, one night, he wrapped his car around a tree. Killed himself and almost killed his best friend, Kenny."

"Does anyone around here know about her past?"

"A few. Jennie wants to live a private life, so I don't advertise why my niece returned to town."

"She seems...scared." He tapped his lower lip. "No, scared isn't right. Make that leery."

Emily opened her mouth then closed it. "I've probably said too much as is. The rest is her story to tell, not mine. But to give you the basics, Zoey stays with me while her mom works, and we get together frequently. It's not a secret, but I try to keep that tidbit to myself for Jennie's sake."

He rubbed the back of his neck and peered at the older woman. "I appreciate everything you've told me. I'd like to ask one more thing."

Mrs. Hanover nodded.

"Is there anyone out there that would want to hurt Jennie or Zoey?"

The older lady stared at the floor for a moment. "Let me just say, not that I know of."

"Miss Emily, that's a bit cagey."

"Well, that's all you're going to get." She stood, putting an end to their conversation. "If you'll excuse me, I need to get ready for my special afternoon guest. And I'd appreciate it if you weren't here when she comes."

"Yes, ma'am. Thank you for your time." He rose to his feet. He'd filled in several holes, only to have a few more questions pop up.

Emily patted his cheek and smiled. "Now, if you decide to come and ask about Jennie on a personal level, I'll be happy to answer your questions."

David's mouth hung open. The woman had the tenacity of a dog with a bone.

She chuckled. "Let me grab you the box of cookies your partner wants."

"How did you know?"

"Oh, please." She disappeared into the kitchen and returned with a container.

"Thank you, Miss Emily."

"You're welcome. Now, scoot." She led him to the door and bid him farewell.

He exited and made his way to his department-issued vehicle. Placing his hand on the driver's side door handle, he shook his head.

Miss Emily had laid down the gauntlet for matchmaking, but he refused to pick it up. He'd failed one woman, and it had cost her her life. He wasn't about to put himself in that situation again.

Besides, he had a crime to investigate. And he refused to allow Zoey to end up as a statistic.

**

"Jennie Rose! Why didn't you tell me what happened last night?"

"Calm down, Aunt Emily. We're fine. It was a mistake, and the police are handling it." Jennie plopped down and folded her arms on the kitchen table. Her shift had ended a little while ago. Grateful for the uneventful day since her mind refused to focus. She'd come straight to Aunt Em's to enjoy her company and pick up Zoey. She hadn't expected an interrogation. "How did you find out?"

Zoey rushed into the room, threw her arms around Jennie, and gave her a big squeeze. "Hi, Mom!" Then she hurried to the living room to finish her homework.

"Hi, honey," Jennie called out after her. Oh, how she missed her baby today. Jennie's imagination had run amok during the day, but seeing her daughter eased the trepidation.

Her gaze floated back to her aunt. "Aunt Em?"

"David Whitman stopped by. Apparently, neither he nor Brandon knew you were my niece. We had a nice chat, and he left. But not before giving me a snapshot of what happened."

Jennie's heart hammered in her chest. She hadn't wanted people to know about her past. She'd paid a horrible price for her stupid mistakes. No need for others to pity her or, even worse, scoff at her poor choices. "What did you tell him?"

"I told him you are family and about Brad's accident."

"What about Kenny?" It was bad enough Detective Whitman knew about her husband's death, but she had no desire for anyone to know about Kenny and the abuse she'd suffered at his hands.

"Of course, I didn't tell him about Kenny. That man can rot in prison for all I care. What he did to you...." Aunt Emily clicked her tongue. "I wish you would have come home and not fallen into that man's arms."

Pink crept up Jennie's cheeks. She'd experienced an enormous loss and found herself pregnant days later, not knowing what to do after her husband's death. Kenny had come to her rescue after recovering from the accident, or so she'd thought, but that was still no excuse for her choices. She'd turned her back on everything her aunt had taught her, and worse yet, she'd turned her back on God. "Choosing to run off with Brad at such an early age...not one of my brightest ideas. Although, he loved me, and I'll never regret having Zoey. But Kenny. . I'm sorry." She shook her head.

"I know you are, honey." Emily smoothed her hand down Jennie's hair. "But you're here now and have straightened out your life. That's all that matters." Em pressed a kiss to the top of her head and scurried back to the stove.

The shame of her decision ten years ago continued to haunt her. Why hadn't she come home to her aunt when her world had fallen apart? If she had, she and Zoey wouldn't have to watch over their shoulders every day.

A tap of the wooden spoon on the edge of the pot heating on the stove pulled Jennie from her musings.

"Have you heard from the handsome detective today?" Aunt Em wiped her hands on her *Kiss the Cook* apron.

Jennie rolled her eyes. The woman was insufferable when it came to her matchmaking tendencies. "No, I haven't. I'm sure he'll call once they have something to report."

As if on cue, her cell phone rang. She glanced at the caller ID. Detective Whitman. Butterflies took flight in her stomach. She'd entered his number into her phone, so she wouldn't miss his call. Only for updates on the creep that had sent the text messages, of course.

She forced her pulse to slow.

This reaction had to stop. Men were off her radar, and she planned to keep it that way.

Taking a deep breath, she answered. "Hello, detective."

"Hi there. Please, call me David."

"All right. David. Do you have any news?" She glanced in her aunt's direction and caught the smirk on the older woman's face. When would Emily learn that Jennie wasn't interested in her aunt's legendary schemes?

"Not a lot." He hesitated. "But I wanted to let you know we cloned Zoey's phone. Thank you for your permission, by the way."

She furrowed her brow. The man knew something. "No problem. I want this guy caught. After this is over, I'll call the cell phone company and change her number."

"Good idea. I'll bring Zoey's phone by later if that's okay. She can have it back, but please let her know we can see all her text messages until you make the change."

"Thank you. I appreciate your honesty. And your help." The one thing her life with Kenny had taught her was the value of the truth. She hated deceitfulness.

Voices hummed in the background. When David returned to their conversation, his words were gentle but clipped. "You're welcome. Listen, Jennie, I'm sorry, but I have to go. Will you be home later tonight?"

"We will. Just give me a quick call before you come. And David?"

"Yes?"

Jennie scraped at a spot on the table with her thumbnail. "Stay safe."

"Thanks."

The line went dead.

She stared at her phone for a moment and sent up a prayer of thanks for placing David and his partner in Zoey's path.

CHAPTER 5

F riday 5:00 p.m.

Tucked in Brandon's spotless sedan, David scanned the area. Fifteen, maybe twenty cars lined the popular general store parking lot. Five or six sported heavily tinted windows.

Those were his targets.

He studied his phone then glanced at his watch, a gift from his late grandfather when he'd graduated from the academy. Shaking it next to his ear, he sighed. Had the timepiece stopped working? Only ten minutes had passed since the last time he'd checked. Cracking the windows an inch hadn't allowed much air flow, but it had helped. He wiped the sweat from his brow, thankful the temperature hadn't spiked. As is, the interior of the car reminded him of a sauna.

"Relax, would ya?" Brandon glared at him. "Just keep monitoring that phone. One of these creeps is bound to open a hotspot soon."

"Not fast enough." David rested his head on the back of his seat. They'd had success before, and he hoped it carried over to today. But until someone in the parking lot opened an access point, they'd have to wait and sweat in Brandon's immaculate vehicle. The man had an OCD tendency when it came to cars, and David feared for his life if he so much as left a piece of trash behind. Okay, maybe not his life, but the idea of a lecture on cleanliness had no appeal.

His partner tapped the steering wheel. "So, what did you find out about our mystery woman?"

"Jennie? Only that she's widowed and Emily Hanover's niece."

Brandon raised an eyebrow.

"Honest. Miss Emily was pretty tight-lipped after spilling the beans about Jennie's deceased husband."

"But you think there's more." Brandon shifted to face David and rested his back against the door.

"Yeah, I do. You saw the panic on her face at the hospital and the look between her and Zoey when we asked if anyone wanted to hurt her. Those aren't the responses of someone at ease and unconcerned."

"I agree. But if this investigation doesn't pan out, we might have to dig into Jennie's background."

David's shoulders slumped. "I hate the thought of treating her like a criminal when she and Zoey are the victims." He glanced at the screen of the phone and straightened. "The hotspot *ILikeChildren* just popped up. Not very subtle, are they?"

"Nope. Never are." Brandon grabbed his small notebook.

David scanned the lot. "I only see four cars occupied. Tag those license plates."

"Got 'em." His partner scribbled down the numbers and lifted his gaze. "Wait. Blue sedan to your left. He's parked at an odd angle. I can't see the plate."

"I'm on it. Be right back." David slipped from the vehicle, clicked the door shut, and edged around several unoccupied cars. Head down, he pretended to text on his phone as he casually waltzed past the vehicle in question. Bingo. His fingers flew over his phone keys, sending the license plate number to Brandon and a request for pick up a block down the street.

Ten minutes later, he dropped into the passenger seat of his partner's car. "Time to run the numbers and pray we get a hit."

With a bit of luck and a lot of divine intervention, the database search would point David in the direction of the disgusting man who attempted to lure in Zoey.

If not, the road to stopping the man could be a long one.

**

Jennie's thundering heart threatened to explode from her chest. The laptop on the kitchen table taunted her. The subject line from an unknown address simply stated *Zoey*. Her finger hovered over the mouse. Should she click and see what waited inside? What if her past had come back to haunt her?

Ridiculous. Kenny had four more years in prison. She'd never understand how the man hadn't received a life sentence. The difference between attempted voluntary manslaughter and murder, she guessed.

She ran her hand under her hair along the base of her neck and lingered on the raised skin that spanned three inches. The contact point of the coffee table's edge on Kenny's initial shove. Her knuckle feathered across her rebuilt cheekbone. The second point of his assault, and the one that mercifully knocked her unconscious before he continued his attack.

How had she allowed him to control her and abuse her like that? He'd isolated her from her friends before she'd known what had happened. Then tore down her fragile self-esteem. In the end, he'd trapped her in his controlling world. If it hadn't been for Tina...

Knock. Knock.

Jennie jumped. Her hand went to her chest, and she spun toward the front door. Sweat beaded on her brow, and her pulse skyrocketed. She closed her eyes and willed her racing mind to settle. Once confident her legs wouldn't buckle, she stood.

"It's not him, you coward. He wouldn't knock." She padded across the wood floor.

A quick peek through the peephole had Jennie breathing a sigh of relief. Detective Whitman stood with his hands in his pockets.

Ever since the text message debacle, she'd watched over her shoulder. It was ludicrous, really. She'd spent the last six years stuffing her fears into a manageable box. Now that the lid had lifted, she had to get a handle on it again. Thank goodness Zoey had spent the night at Aunt Em's. Her daughter didn't need to see her freaking out like this.

She edged the door open. "David?"

"Sorry I didn't call. Between a stake out and being a twelve-year-old girl, I lost track of time."

"Huh?" She scrunched her forehead.

"Professional hazard." The sheepish expression on his face made her smile.

Her mind latched onto his meaning. She leaned against the doorframe and tilted her head. "Is that how you find the predators?"

"One way. Anyway, sorry for not calling." He glanced around the yard. "Mind if I come in?"

"Now it's my turn to apologize. Please." She made a sweeping motion, inviting him into the house. "Make yourself at home. Can I get you anything?"

"No, I'm fine." The man lowered himself onto the couch and studied her. "Are you okay? You seem a bit shaken."

Did she dare tell him? What if he thought she overreacted? But from everything she'd learned about David, he was nothing like Kenny. He wouldn't demean her. Wouldn't hit her. She hoped. "I-I received an email earlier. It...surprised me." Her gaze darted to her laptop on the kitchen table. "I haven't opened it yet, but that can wait."

He cocked an eyebrow.

She ignored his silent question, sat on the other side of the sofa, and clutched her hands together. "Do you have news?" Oh, how she hoped they had the evil man behind bars.

"Some. We think we've narrowed it down to two or three guys."

"Really? How?" Hope sparked. Once they caught the child predator, she'd be able to breathe. At least on that front.

"These perverted men are known to share pictures online through hotspots in store parking lots."

Bile rose in her throat. Young girls' pictures online? For others to see? She swallowed. "How do you know it's them?"

"They aren't secretive. The SSIDs they use are...let's just say they're disgusting at times."

"Can't you follow their IP addresses or something?" She was unsure how all of that worked, but she'd heard the term before. Man, she hoped she didn't sound stupid.

"I wish. They use multiple burner phones. They aren't the sharpest tools in the shed, but they aren't dumb either."

Reality hit Jennie like a brick to the head. Her heart raced, and black dots pricked her vision. She inhaled through her nose and blew out air through her pursed lips. "You mean my daughter's picture could be out there for every child predator to see?" And what about Kenny? Had this led him to her doorstep?

David tucked his chin to his chest. "Unfortunately, yes."

Blood whooshed in her ears. Had a mistaken text message revealed her location? One she'd tried hard to keep private.

She stood and wrapped her arms around her waist and paced the room. "This can't be happening."

**

"I wish I had a different answer, but I don't." Something about this woman's vulnerability tugged at David's heart. He physically hurt for Zoey's mother. He stayed seated and watched her move back and forth across the room.

"I've been so careful." Tears trailed down Jennie's cheeks. "We love it here," she whispered.

Wait. What? Why did she have to be careful? Based on the reaction he'd witnessed and her secretive nature, the detective in him said that her husband had abused her, but he'd died before Zoey's birth. Jennie had never mentioned anyone else in her life except Miss Emily and her friend Tina. Which in and of itself struck him as strange.

David rose and gently held her shoulders. "Jennie, what's going on?"

"I thought—never mind." She swiped at the wetness on her face. "So now what happens?"

Jennie held tight to the private information she harbored, no doubt about that. He'd let her keep it for now. But sooner or later, he'd get to the bottom of whatever had panicked her.

"We'll continue to investigate. Background checks and further communication should lead us in the right direction. Plus, we have a secret weapon. Megan, our tech guru, is incredible at her job. The team won't stop until we figure it out."

"Promise?" Jennie's eyes held so much hope that the look almost brought him to his knees.

He longed to give her guarantees, but no one could. And he refused to lie to her. The world was full of evil—he should know. His fiancée had died at the hands of evil. "I promise we'll do our best."

She nodded. Her eyes shifted to the kitchen table and back to him.

He followed her gaze. "Is there something I should know?"

Her mouth twisted to the side, and she scrunched her forehead.

Come on, Jennie. Let me into your world. I want to help you.

She inhaled, stepped from his grasp, and retrieved her computer. "I was about to open this email when you knocked." She lowered herself onto the couch.

David sat beside her and peered over her shoulder. His gut clenched when he read the subject line. Zoey.

Her hand shook as she clicked on the message. One by one, image after image loaded onto the page. Jennie gasped.

Five photos jumped from the screen. Two pictures zoomed in on Zoey's face while she played at recess, and three more of Jennie and Zoey in front of the school filled the display.

"Those are from today! Why? Who?" Jennie squeaked.

David rested his hands on the cushion behind her. "It appears whoever did this isn't solely focused on Zoey."

Jennie stared at the photos.

Could it be possible that someone from her past had come back to scare her—or worse? It made no sense. David rubbed the back of his neck. The man they hunted wouldn't have switched his attention to Jennie. The creep would only have eyes for a young girl. A fact that continued to churn his stomach after three years of being a member of the ICAC task force.

"Forward that email to me, please. I'd like Megan to see if she can glean anything from those photos." He rattled off his email address.

"Of course." Jennie fired off the email then slammed her laptop shut. "I can't believe this."

"We'll get to the bottom of it." He resisted placing his hands on her shoulders as his mind raced with possibilities.

"How can you say that? You can't promise you'll catch this guy." She peered up at him, her words holding no contempt. Only sadness.

"I'll do my best, Jennie. I won't let some maniac hurt you or Zoey." He shifted to her side. "I seem to have acquired a soft spot for that girl of yours." *And you.* When he'd met her forty-eight hours ago, the wall he'd built around his heart after his fiancée Brenda's death had cracked. Pieces had begun to chip away. He didn't understand how it happened, but it had.

She looked at him with such desperation. "We have for you, too." Her eyes widened. "I mean, *she* has for you."

His lips twitched, but he held the smile at bay. And to think he'd been concerned the attraction was one-sided. He reached to tuck a strand of hair behind her ear but dropped his hand to his side. He hadn't earned the right to touch her yet. Besides, if he allowed his feelings to take root, he'd only fail her like he'd failed Brenda.

Friends. He could do friends. Decision made. He exhaled. "I need to get going. Are you going to be okay here by yourself?"

"I'll be fine. I know you must be tired. Go home and get some rest." She smiled, but it didn't reach her eyes.

Tired didn't come close. David's twenty-hour day had him weary to the bone. "Lock up behind me." Forgetting the words of wisdom to himself, he scooped her hand into his and squeezed her fingers. Her soft skin, a contrast to his callouses. His pulse quickened at the touch. "I don't want you taking any chances."

Tears filled her eyes. She nodded.

The protector in him wanted to pull her into a hug and hold her until her fears dissipated, but he refused to accidentally trigger bad memories for her.

"Let me know if there's anything I can do." He ducked his head and peered into her eyes. "Anything." Opening the front door, he stepped onto the porch and turned in time to watch the door close behind him.

He waited until he heard all three locks click into place, then scanned the yard and the neighboring houses.

Thirteen years of experience as a cop had the hairs on the back of his neck tingling. His hand hovered over his holster as he descended the steps. Removing the phone from his pocket with his other hand, he placed a call to his partner.

Brandon answered on the second ring. "What's up?"

"Send extra patrols by Jennie Nielson's tonight."

"Hold on." A moment later, Brandon returned. "Done. Why?"

David stood at the driver's side of his vehicle, staring at Jennie's house. Maybe paranoia had snuck in, but he refused to ignore his instincts. The one time he'd discounted the internal urges to stop working and go help Brenda, his fiancée had paid the price. "My gut."

"Good enough for me."

David released the breath he hadn't known he'd held. "Thanks, man. I'll see you in the morning."

"I'm guessing you haven't checked your messages."

"Nope. I haven't had time."

"Since our case is at a standstill until Megan does her mojo, the lieutenant told everyone to go to on-call and take the weekend off. Guess he has a heart, after all."

David laughed. "Not hardly. The man doesn't want us on overtime."

Brandon snorted. "You're probably right about that. Either way, I'm going to enjoy the extra sleep."

"You and me both, buddy." David tapped the hood of his car. "Go home."

"Copy that." The phone went dead.

Guess he didn't have to tell his partner twice.

His gaze roamed the area. Lots of places to hide, but at least Jennie's neighbor had dogs.

When the lights went out in her living room, he slipped into the sedan and started the engine. He laid his head back on the headrest and prayed that whatever truth Jennie continued to hide wouldn't get her hurt or, worse yet, killed.

***

Jennie had flipped the deadbolts and turned out the lights. Resting her forehead against the cool wood of the door, she allowed tears to fall. How had her life taken another wrong turn?

God, haven't I suffered enough?

But God wasn't to blame. She'd caused her own misery.

She should've told David about Kenny, but what were the odds the man who'd almost taken her life was out of prison, much less could find her and torment her or Zoey. A child predator definitely didn't describe Kenny. A control freak. A narcissist. A man who thought he owned women—Yes. But during the four years they'd lived together, he never touched Zoey other than to hug her. He'd only abused Jennie when she disobeyed him.

If it wasn't Kenny, then who?

Bile rose in her throat at the thought of Zoey having a stalker. And what was she going to do about David? She'd vowed to never let another man into her life. But in the short time she'd known the handsome detective, the man had wormed his way into her thoughts.

He had her stomach tied in knots. His nearness made her nerves tingle. She'd wanted to throw herself into his arms tonight for comfort, but she'd made enough mistakes to last a lifetime. She had no business getting involved with another man. If she were smart, she'd stay far away from the entire species. At least when it came to relationships.

Since David came into her life, the old desire for companionship tugged at her. Her deceased husband might have been a drunk, but he'd loved her and never hurt her. He'd never talked to her like she was beneath him. Brad's flaw—when he drank, he drank to excess. He was a danger and an embarrassment to himself and those around him. But he'd never been violent. She'd loved the man despite his faults.

After her husband died and she'd given birth to Zoey, single motherhood became overwhelming, and she'd lost her confidence and ability to cope with life. Brad's friends Levi and Adam tried to help in their own way, but it had been his best friend Kenny who had convinced her to move in and look where that had gotten her. After multiple trips to the hospital, she'd finally ended up in the ICU, and him in jail.

Never again would she allow herself to be vulnerable and give up control of her life to a man. To anyone, for that matter. She only trusted God. The shame of her decisions and the fear of dying at Kenny's hands had forced her to face her mistakes and ask God for forgiveness. He'd given her five years of peace. She should be thankful, but she couldn't help wondering why He'd allowed pain into her life again.

She exhaled, picked up her phone from the end table, and called Aunt Emily. Relief filled her that Zoey stayed with her aunt, but concern continued to strangle Jennie. She had to warn Aunt Em to be on alert for anything strange while caring for Zoey.

"Hello?"

"Aunt Em, how are things going?" Jennie flipped on the nightlight in the kitchen on her way to the bedroom. A requirement for her sanity after her final hospital stay.

"Fine, honey. Zoey's in bed reading. Do you need to talk with her?"

"No. No. I called to ask you to keep a close eye on her while she's with you." She stepped across the threshold of her bedroom and froze. She scanned her room. Her gaze landed on the closed closet door. She gripped the phone tighter. Her hands trembled.

"Of course. What's going on, Jennie?" Aunt Em's words broke through her terror.

No use hiding what happened from the older woman. She'd discover the truth in minutes if she set her mind to it. The police should hire the woman to interrogate criminals. They'd spill their secrets before she finished saying hello.

Jennie sighed. "Someone emailed pictures of Zoey and me. Pictures we didn't know the person had taken." Her steps faltered the closer she got to the closet door.

"How awful. Did you call Detective Whitman? Would you like to spend the night here?"

Jennie held her breath and opened the door. She swiped her clothes to the side. Empty. She closed her eyes and took a deep breath.

"Jennie?"

She shook her head. "Sorry. I'm still here. No, I'm good, and David knows. Could you keep Zoey until late-morning since she doesn't have school tomorrow? I know how she loves her baking time with you."

"Sounds good, honey. Take care of yourself. Come over if you need to."

"I will. Thanks again for everything, Aunt Em."

"Love you, sweetie."

"Love you too." She tapped the end button on her phone and placed it on her dresser. Her emerald heart pendant necklace that Kenny had given her lay in a swirl next to her jewelry box. She furrowed her brow. Hadn't she disposed of that piece of jewelry before she'd moved? Maybe Tina had packed it, not realizing where it had come from. But still, why was it out?

Zoey. Her shoulders relaxed. It had to have been Zoey. She'd ask her daughter about it tomorrow.

Jennie chucked the necklace into the trashcan. After one last look around, she changed into her pajamas and crawled into bed.

Her skin prickled, and her gaze darted to each corner of the room. Something triggered her anxiety. But what? She scrambled out of bed, retrieved her phone, then returned and pulled the covers to her chin.

Her fingers itched to call David, but she had to be strong. She refused to show weakness. Refused to let someone control her ever again.

The curtains hung motionless. Her dresser knickknacks all in place. The teddy bear Tina had bought her during her hospital stay sat on the chair in the corner. Nothing appeared out of place except the necklace she'd thought she'd thrown out years ago.

See, no reason to panic.

She would not let fear win.

The claws of doubt grabbed ahold and dug in.

Would her stubbornness get her killed?

CHaPTer 6

Saturday 11:00 a.m.

David's feet pounded in the soft dirt along the edge of the lake. His tender ankle ached and the sweat trickling down his arm burned his stitches. The late start to his morning had delayed his jog. He almost threw his running shoes back into his closet, but with his thoughts cluttered from the events of the past few days, he knew exercise would clear the cobwebs.

His rhythmic breathing held cadence while his mind swirled. Last night when he'd stared into Jennie's deep blue eyes, his heart betrayed him. He'd vowed to keep his distance from any relationship until he left the law enforcement profession. That way, when he failed to keep the woman he loved safe, he wouldn't feel like a complete failure.

Brenda's death weighed on him. It had been his fault. No one could tell him different.

Wrong place, wrong time. You didn't cause it. The statement his captain had told him had haunted him for the past two years.

Of course, it was his fault. If he'd only left work to help her instead of staying at the office and finishing his report... Since that moment, he'd turned into a control freak. At least according to Brandon.

He increased his speed. The pain in his ankle screamed at him, but he deserved it.

"Detective?" A young voice drifted through the air.

He slowed to a stop and put his hands on his knees, sucking air as he glanced in the direction of the summons.

An energetic ten-year-old jumped up and sprinted toward him. He looked past Zoey and there sat the gorgeous woman he'd dreamt about all night. He smiled and waved.

He peeled his gaze from Jennie seconds before Zoey barreled into him, throwing her arms around his waist.

"Detective Whitman." She grinned up at him.

"You can call me David if it's okay with your momma." He slipped his arms around her and squeezed.

"Hmm. I better go with Mr. David so Momma doesn't get upset with me."

"Fine by me." He released her and mussed the top of her head.

Zoey giggled.

"So, Squirt, what are you doing out here?"

Hands on her hips, she glared at him. But the small upward curve of her lips told him she liked the nickname.

"Momma and I brought a picnic lunch and a Frisbee." She slid her tiny hand into his.

"Sounds like an awesome plan." He herded Zoey toward the blanket where Jennie sat.

"We just finished, but there are leftovers if you want some." Energy bubbled from the young girl.

Oh, to be ten again. "Thanks, Zoey, that's nice of you to offer." His stomach would appreciate the food, but he didn't want to intrude. "Let's go say hi to your mom."

Sunrays filtered through the wispy clouds and bounced off Jennie's blonde hair, giving her a halo. The angelic vision stole his breath. He halted mid-stride.

"Mr. David? You okay?" Zoey tugged his hand.

"I'm good." A flash of light caught his attention. He held his hand to his forehead and shielded his eyes.

His heart pounded in his chest. He bolted toward the unsuspecting woman on the blanket. "Jennie!"

She stood and stared at him.

Several small boulders tumbled down the hill from the parking lot, causing a landslide of stones. Jennie and Zoey's picnic spot directly in the path of the rocks.

God, please don't let me too late. "Zoey, get out of here! Jennie, run!"

Jennie sprinted toward him.

He grabbed her, threw her to the ground, and covered her with his body.

Screams filled his ears.

Pieces of debris showered over David's back and legs. Sharp pricks and hard hits cut and bruised his skin.

When the fragments of the hillside settled, he inhaled. Pain sliced through him and a moan escaped as he rolled to the side, allowing Jennie room to breathe.

"Are you hurt?" She scrambled to her knees and leaned over him. Her warm breath feathered across his face.

He closed his eyes, willing the aches to subside. "I'm okay." He blinked and focused on Jennie.

Blood covered her lower lip, and a red mark marred her cheek.

He pushed himself to a seated position and swiped the red liquid from her mouth with the pad of his thumb. His stomach twisted. "You're injured."

"Don't worry about me. You're the one who needs medical attention." She sat back on her heels and shifted her gaze to Zoey who stood twenty feet away. "Honey, call 911."

David shook his head. "I don't need an ambulance, but we do need the police."

"What? Why?" She stared at him.

He captured her fingers. "Those rocks didn't fall down the embankment by themselves. Someone caused the initial slide."

"How do you know?" She brushed a loose strand of hair from her forehead with a shaky hand.

"I saw a figure at the edge of the parking lot just as the small boulder started to roll."

"Doesn't mean they were pushed."

"Maybe not, but the person ran away."

Jennie huffed and stood. She held her arms open and Zoey dove into her embrace.

"Are you okay, Momma?"

"I'm fine, sweetie. I have a first-aid kit in my bag. Go get it for me."

Zoey rushed over, grabbed the bag, and returned.

"Thanks, Zoe." Jennie circled behind him. "Let's take a look at the damage."

"You don't—"

"Don't have to? Yeah, I know, but I'm a nurse and you're hurt. It's what I do. Besides, you protected me." Kneeling behind him, she helped him off with his shirt and sucked in a sharp breath.

"That doesn't sound good?" He glanced over his shoulder.

"You look as if you met up with Freddy Krueger." Her fingers feathered his ripped skin.

He hissed. "I figured the cuts would be a nice addition to my sliced arm."

"Not funny." Jennie tore open a package and dabbed his wounds.

"No, it's not. Someone's out to hurt you."

She continued to treat his back. "Are you sure it wasn't just an accident?"

Had it been a mishap? The odds were against it, but still... "It's possible, I suppose."

"We'll tell the officers what happened and see if they find any evidence proving your theory." Jennie handed him his shirt. "All done. Be sure to get those cuts nice and clean when you get home. I don't want to see you at the hospital with an infection." She stood and held out her hand.

Zoey joined her mom with the offer to help him stand.

He placed his hands in theirs and forced himself to his feet. "Thanks, ladies."

Zoey threw her arms around his waist. "Thank you for saving my mom."

David rubbed the girls back.

A blue and white police cruiser parked at the top of the hill.

He squinted in the direction of the officer making his way down the steps on the far side and smiled. "Let's go say hi to Officers Hanes."

Jennie and Zoey walked alongside him toward his brother in blue. "Hey, Randy."

"How's it going, man?"

"Been better." David wanted to talk with the officer out of earshot of Zoey, but the young girl was too perceptive and seemed wise beyond her years. He'd wondered about her maturity when he'd first met her, but he hadn't figured out why yet. "I'd like to introduce you to Jennie and Miss Zoey."

Hanes tipped a pretend hat. "Ladies. Want to tell me what happened?" The officer pulled a pen and pad of paper from his pocket and motioned toward a metal picnic table several yards away.

The small group trudged over and plopped down. The adrenaline had faded, and fatigue settled in.

David ran his hand through his hair and proceeded to give Officer Hanes his account of the near tragedy. Jennie and Zoey added their statement to his while Hanes took notes and appeared concerned with the information.

"I'll take a look up top and see if the stranger left behind any evidence of foul play." Hanes stood and shook David's hand. "I'll get back to you with my findings."

"I appreciate it." David glanced at Jennie. "Are you ready to go home or do you plan to stay?"

"I think we've had enough for today. We'll head back to the house and find something to do to keep our minds off what happened."

He hesitated. "Would you mind if I rode with you, then ran home from your house. It would make me feel better knowing you made it home."

Jennie bit her lower lip then nodded.

He placed his hand over hers. "Thank you." He'd tuck her safely into her cottage before he ran home, took a shower, and called his partner.

Things had hit weird status. His mind spun with the events of the last hours.

Was Jennie the target of something sinister? Or had he seen things that weren't there and the rocks had fallen by themselves?

His gut told him to keep an eye on the pretty blonde sitting across from him. He refused to fail her and add to his guilt.

CHAPTER 7

S unday 2:00 p.m.

Sunday afternoon, Jennie played the beach scene over and over in her head. It hadn't helped her worry when David called her multiple times after he'd seen her home and deemed her little house safe. What if the landslide hadn't been an accident like he thought? But why?

"Momma?" Zoey tugged on Jennie's shirttail.

The mixer hummed and her daughter held out a spatula.

Jennie blinked. "I'm sorry, baby." She took the offered utensil and scraped the sides of the bowl containing the start of chocolate chip cookies.

"Ready?" Zoey hovered a measuring cup above the egg and sugar blend.

"Got for it."

Zoey peered into the bowl. A dusting of flour poofed in her face. The girl giggled.

She smiled at her ten-year-old. So innocent, yet wiser than most adults. Her smile faded. Due to her poor choices, her daughter had lost her carefree childhood.

The two finished with the dough and placed a cookie sheet filled with lumps of yummy goodness into the oven. Jennie set a timer and washed her hands.

The doorbell buzzed and Zoey sprinted for the front entrance.

Her heartbeat thundered in her chest. "Zoey! Wait!" Visions of the creep who'd texted her whirled in her mind. What if he'd come to take her daughter?

She threw the cloth she'd used to dry her hands on the table and raced after Zoey.

"Aunt Tina!" Zoey squealed with delight.

Jennie rounded the corner in time to see Zoey jump into her best friend's arms.

"How's my girl?" Tina squeezed the young girl, dropped her to her feet, and stepped back, keeping her hands on Zoey's shoulders. "Let me look at you. You've gotten so big. What's your mother feeding you?"

"Vegetables." Her daughter screwed up her face. "Yuck."

Tina laughed. She placed her hand next to her mouth and whispered loud enough for Jennie to hear. "I agree."

"Stop conspiring with my kid." Jennie grinned.

Her friend's gaze connected with hers. Two years had passed since they'd seen each other in person. They video chatted frequently, but Tina had kept her distance for Jennie's sake. Her fear of being found had dictated their agreement.

So why had Tina come now?

She embraced the woman who'd befriended her during the darkest years of her life. The woman who'd discovered her battered body and had taken care of her little girl while she'd fought for her life in the ICU. A woman whom she loved like a sister.

"I've missed you." Tears welled in Jennie's eyes.

"Me too."

After the long hug, Jennie ushered Tina to the living room and motioned for her to have a seat.

Jennie plopped down on the sofa opposite Tina. Zoey had managed to wiggle between them. "Not that I'm not thrilled to see you, but what are you doing here?"

Tina's gaze connected with Zoey's.

Hmm. Something was up with those two.

"All right you two sp—"

The kitchen timer rang.

Jennie jumped from the couch. "The cookies. I'll be right back." She paused and glared at the pair. "Don't think you guys are off the hook." She rushed to the kitchen and removed the baking sheets. Placing them on the counter to cool, she hurried back to her friend.

Stepping into the living room, she stopped. Zoey and Tina talked in hushed tones. Her friend's deep brown complexion contrasted with Zoey's lighter features. The two were completely opposite in looks, but exactly the same in personality. And a force to be reckoned with when they were together. Jennie was in trouble if these two were plotting. What were they up to now?

When they noticed her, they stopped.

"I can see there's a conspiracy going on. Spill it." Jennie lowered herself onto the couch.

Zoey snuggled beside her. "I love you, Momma."

She raised a brow. "Uh huh."

"Forget it, Zoe. We've been found out." Tina turned her attention to Jennie. "Zoey called me yesterday."

Her friend held up her hand to stave off the comment Jennie had on the tip of her tongue.

"She told me about the text message and the weird stuff going on, including yesterday's incident. Girl, I'm worried. I had to come. Please let me stay and help."

Jennie rubbed her forehead with her thumb and forefinger. "I..." What could she say? Worry consumed her that Zoey's predator would find her. And then there was David. Tina would have plenty to say about that. But as much as she tried to be independent, she needed her friend. "I suppose you two will wear me down, and I'll end up agreeing anyway." Jennie gave

Tina a genuine smile. Not a forced one she'd become good at over the last couple of days. "You can stay."

Zoey leapt from her seat and fist bumped Tina. "I knew she wouldn't tell us no."

"You and me both." Tina wrapped her arm around Zoey's waist and the two formed a united front.

The doorbell rang for a second time. Jennie's peaceful haven had turned into Grand Central Station.

"Who on earth could that be?" She stood and pinned her daughter with a glare. "You didn't summon anyone else, did you?"

Zoey raised her hands in surrender and shot her a *who me?* expression.

Jennie exhaled. She hoped whoever her daughter had contacted didn't turn her world upside down.

She turned the knob and eased open the door.

Detective Whitman stood on the porch in worn jeans and a black t-shirt, highlighting muscles she'd tried to ignore since they'd first met.

Jennie fisted her hands on her hips. "So, what line did Zoey feed you to get you to come over?"

His eyebrow arched. "Excuse me?"

"It seems as though my daughter is calling in back up. Just wondering how she got you here."

The corner of his lips curved upward as he propped himself on the doorframe. "Well, let me see. She did promise me cookies."

"She did not." She narrowed her gaze. The man was enjoying her frustration.

"Okay, she didn't. But they smell good." He grinned like a little boy.

She shook her head and stepped aside. "Come on in, join the party."

He brushed past her. "Party? What party?" He froze. "I'm sorry. You have company. I can come back later."

"No." Zoey rushed to David. Grabbing his hand, she pulled him the rest of the way into the room. "I want you to meet my Aunt Tina. Well, she isn't really my aunt, but that's what I call her. She's mom's best friend...and mine too." Her daughter beamed at Tina.

Tina rose and extended her hand. "I'm Tina."

"David." He accepted her offered hand. "Ahh, so you're Aunt Tina. Nice to meet you."

Her friend perused David from head to toe. "You're right, Zoey. He *is* hot."

David choked and coughed.

Jennie patted him on the back. "Sorry about that, but you'll have to get used to it. Tina is nothing if not blunt."

"I...um...thanks...I think," he stammered.

Laughter bubbled from Jennie. She wondered how often David found himself speechless. "Go on. Have a seat. She's harmless."

His eyes widened. "Are you sure about that?"

"Most of the time." She motioned him toward the easy chair. The least she could do was give him a safe place to sit. She plopped on the sofa near Tina. "What brings you by?" She shifted her gaze to her daughter, then back to the man trying to compose himself.

He cleared his throat. "I came from talking with Officer Hanes about yesterday's incident. The evidence is inconclusive. The small boulders could have been pushed causing the rock-slide, but they didn't find anything to say one way or the other."

Her shoulders slumped. "Then I'm thinking positive. It was a mishap."

David leaned forward and rested his forearms on his knees. "I want to agree with you, but I can't ignore what I saw."

"What you saw?" Tina piped in.

"Right before the rocks tumbled toward Jennie, someone was watching from the top of the hill." David ran a hand over his head, mussing his hair. "I'm sorry I failed. I should have focused harder and got a better look at him. Then we'd know for sure."

"Failed?" Zoey shot off the couch, her voice rose an octave. "You yelled at my momma. Then tackled her, protecting her like some sort of superhero. Who cares what the person looked like? Momma didn't get hurt because of you."

Jennie clasped her daughter's hand and pulled. "Honey."

"Well, it's true," Zoey huffed and dropped beside her.

"I agree with my daughter. You saved me from being hurt or worse." She rubbed Zoey's back but never took her gaze off David. "Speaking of hurt. How are the cuts and bruises?"

He blinked as if hers and Zoey's words didn't compute. "I'm a bit sore, but ibuprofen is doing the trick. By the way, thanks for taking care of my wounds."

"It's what I do." The words left her mouth before she could haul them back in. The man had risked greater injuries in his attempt to shield her. "It was the least I could do. You protected me and got hurt doing so."

Hair sticking out in multiple directions, he stared at her then sighed. "Listen, I should head out. I only wanted to give you the info in person." He pinned his gaze on Zoey. "Sorry I couldn't confirm whether or not the rocks were an accident. But I'll keep looking into it."

Jennie's daughter nodded. The movement almost imperceptible. What was going on between those two?

David slapped his legs and stood. "I better go."

"Hold on." Zoey hurried to the kitchen.

He turned to face Jennie. "Sorry for the interruption."

"It wasn't a problem. Besides, I have a feeling someone in this house knew you were coming."

"Maybe." He grinned.

Zoey appeared in the living room. "Here." She shoved a paper plate at him. "I want you to have some cookies."

Hand on her daughter's shoulder, David closed his eyes and exhaled. "Thank you." He peered at Jennie. "I'll let you catch up with Tina."

The man's tenderness toward Zoey and his protective nature yesterday had her mind swirling. She'd only known him a few days, but he exuded integrity. Plus, Aunt Emily trusted him. Could she?

He pivoted and was gone before she untangled her thoughts.

She stood staring at the wooden barrier between her and the man who'd saved her life.

"You're right, Zoe." Tina's voice broke through her musing.

"Told you," her daughter sang.

Jennie spun and faced her friend and daughter. "What are you talking about?"

"Nothing," they said in unison.

Yeah, right. Those two were trouble with a capital T.

"What do you say we get a snack and have a marathon chat session?"

Tina smiled. "I'd love it."

Six hours later, Zoey headed off to bed, leaving Jennie draped over the arms of the easy chair and Tina sprawled across the couch.

Jennie had missed her friend, but her life was different than when she lived next to Tina. The woman had been her lifeline and had begged her to walk away from Kenny.

"I've never thanked you for being there for me. If I'd only listened to you sooner."

"You were hurting and scared. Everyone could see that."

"I think all of Brad's friends felt bad for me. Levi and Adam stopped by Kenny's and checked on me every week, sometimes more. Not sure Kenny was too happy about it, but he put up with it."

"Levi and Adam have asked about you over the years, especially this last month. I've never hinted that we keep in touch or where you live which didn't make them happy. They both worry about you."

"I miss those two. They weren't only Brad's friends but mine too." Tina's words registered. Jennie scrunched her forehead. "Wait. Why this month?"

"You haven't heard?" Tina's eyes widened. "You haven't, have you?"

"What are you talking about?"

Tina flung her legs over the edge of the cushions and sat up. "Kenny had his parole hearing a week ago."

The world spun and the lights grew dim. He couldn't be out. The man had beaten her and left her for dead. If Tina hadn't found her... She pulled in a ragged breath, "Was he released?"

Her friend nodded. "I thought you knew."

"No. I've had no contact from my old life except for you. I didn't leave my address with the police either. I hadn't wanted to take a chance." She scrubbed her hands over her face.

"Levi visited Kenny in prison over the years, said he'd changed. Felt bad for how he'd treated you. Even had a groupie girlfriend that he was looking forward to being with once he was out."

"Does Levi believe him? Do you believe him?" Jennie's stomach twisted in knots. The man who'd almost killed her was back on the streets. Had he found her? Was he the one causing all the problems?

"Not sure on both accounts. Levi seemed to think he still has anger issues so he's leery of Kenny's proclamation. Adam on the other hand thought Kenny told the truth."

Jennie's heart raced. This couldn't be happening. She bolted to the door and checked the locks.

"What if it was him at the lake? What if he was the one who tried to hurt me?"

She thought she had more time. Her worst nightmare was on the loose.

CHAPTER 8

Monday 7:00 a.m.

Cup of dark brew in hand, David inhaled the rich bold aroma and closed his heavy eyelids. The hum of voices and activity of the coffee shop faded into the background. After visiting Jennie on Sunday afternoon, David had spent the evening and all night playing the evidence in Zoey's case over in his head. But it was the email Jennie had forwarded to him that confused him the most. Nothing pointed to anyone other than a pedophile. So why had the creep included Jennie in the last three of the photos?

There was only one answer. A different person other than the one from the mistaken text stalked the pair.

Then the weekend incident happened. Maybe it had been just an accident, but he couldn't shake the feeling that someone had intended to harm her. His shoulders slumped at the thought. Lack of sleep was catching up with him. During college, an all-nighter wouldn't have fazed him. But over a decade later, his body didn't recover as easily.

He took a sip and blinked, bringing the world into focus. His tired gaze spotted Brandon heading his way, appearing as frazzled as David.

David sat his mug on the table. "Hey, partner. You look about as good as I feel. The twins keep you up late last night? Or did you have a hot date?"

Brandon plopped onto the bench opposite David in the corner booth and scowled at him. "You think I have time to date with Katie and Kyle taking up all my energy and brain cells? Those kids of mine decided last night would be a good night to break curfew and waltzed in an hour late."

David chuckled. "They're a handful. Always into mischief and sticking up for each other."

"Yeah, the twins insist on doing things together. They're even double dating so I can't get mad at just one of them." The corners of Brandon's lips curved downward.

"You miss her, don't you?" David hadn't known Brandon's late wife, Tish, but if his partner's admiration of her was any indication, the woman had been amazing.

"Every day." Brandon swiped his hand over his tired face and inhaled. "So, what's new with the case?"

David placed his hand on the folder sitting next to his placemat and slid it toward Brandon. "Jennie received an email Friday night. Those were in it."

The waitress sat a mug of coffee in front of Brandon and poured David a second cup.

Once the woman sauntered away, his partner opened the file. He gave a low whistle through his teeth. "Huh. Not what I expected."

"Me either. I was pretty sure Zoey's picture would be out on the web, but Zoey and Jennie together? Makes me wonder."

"Exactly. This isn't the same man who communicated with Zoey." Brandon's gaze met his. "You tell Jennie, yet?"

"No. Haven't had the opportunity. I was a little busy helping her dodge falling boulders on Saturday. Besides, I wanted to study the photos before I came to any conclusions."

"You better tell her, or something tells me she'll bite your head off if she finds out you're hiding something from her."

David lifted his mug and saluted Brandon. "Right you are."

"By the way, how's she doing?" Brandon slid his cup in a circle on the table.

"It shook her up a bit, but she's tough."

"What about you? How's your arm and back?"

"Not gonna lie, I'm sore, but it could have been a lot worse." His skin burned where the cuts rubbed against his shirt. Living alone had its drawbacks, one being no one to help with unreachable places.

"Very true." His partner tipped his mug, emptied it, then raised it to the waitress.

The server placed a coffee pot on the table. "There ya go, boys. You look like you need it."

"Thanks," they said in unison as she walked away.

The two continued to update each other on their open cases and status of the current search warrant requests. Several cups of coffee later and their task list ready for action, a flit of blonde hair captured David's attention. Jennie stood at the entrance, scanning the room. He narrowed his gaze. The dark circles under the woman's eyes and her drooped shoulders concerned him.

Brandon shifted and looked around the edge of the booth. "Ah, my signal to leave."

"You don't have to..."

His partner waved his hand at him. "I've got to get busy anyway. And you have information to share with a very tired looking young lady."

"You noticed that too, eh?"

"Hard to miss." Brandon slid from the seat. "See ya later."

Jennie said hello to Brandon on his way out then her eyes met David's. She ambled to his table.

"Please. Have a seat." He motioned to the bench Brandon had vacated.

"Thank you." Jennie lowered herself to the seat and in one graceful movement slid her legs under the table.

"Coffee?"

"Yes, please." She tucked a strand of loose hair behind her ear.

David motioned the waitress for another cup. "Where's your friend?"

"Tina's at my place. She had work to do. As a graphic designer, she can work from anywhere. I'm heading home after I run a few errands."

"She seems nice."

"Very much so. I don't think I would have survived my past if it hadn't been for her."

He pondered her statement. It only confirmed she continued to hide something from him.

Jennie exhaled. Her entire body slumped.

"Looks like you had a long night."

Her eyebrow rose.

He sighed. *Smooth, dude.* "I meant you look tired."

She busied herself with unrolling her silverware. "You could say that."

The waitress brought a fresh cup, pouring Jennie's coffee, then hurried to her next customer.

Jennie added a small amount of cream into her cup and stirred the brown liquid.

"Want to talk about it?" He studied her as she tapped her spoon against the edge of her mug then lifted it to take a sip. He waited, giving her time to decide if she wanted to share what had kept her awake last night. Would she finally trust him with her fears and concerns?

She propped her elbows on the table and smiled, but it didn't reach her eyes. "I couldn't sleep." She gripped the cup in front of her tight enough her fingers turned white.

"Any particular reason?"

Her hands trembled causing her coffee to slosh She placed the mug on the table and tucked her hands beneath her legs.

His gut twisted at the pain and uncertainty that swam in her eyes.

***

Of all the places in Pinewood Shores Jennie had to come for coffee, she had to pick this one. David was too perceptive for his own good. She had a decision to make. A hard one.

"Other than the close call with the rocks, I-I found..." She swallowed past the lump in her throat. She should tell him what Tina had said, but Kenny couldn't be behind any of this. He didn't know where she lived. Did he? "I was worried about the pictures in the email. I want my daughter safe and not out there for public consumption."

David's scrutinizing gaze had her squirming in her seat.

She'd mastered a poker face years ago, but lying was a different story. Oh, she could do it, but it wasn't something that had ever come easy. Even when it meant the difference between pain and peace. Besides, David was too perceptive for her to get away with it.

"Jennie." His voice lowered. "Please, trust me."

She sighed. Maybe she'd give him a smidge of the truth and see how he reacted. Grabbing her mug, she stared at the brew. "Zoey found an old necklace of mine and left it on my dresser."

He laid his hand on her forearm. "An old necklace wouldn't have your face drained of all color."

"You're right. It's a reminder of a bad time in my life. I thought I'd gotten rid of it, apparently not, and Zoey must have found it."

His gaze reached down into her heart. He waited. Didn't ask a question. Didn't rush her. Just waited.

Inhaling, she continued. "I never wanted to see it again. It shook me, but I'm okay now. It's gone and I don't ever have to set eyes on it again."

He nodded then removed his hand and rubbed the back of his neck.

Now it was her turn to ask the questions. "What's wrong, David. Why do you look like you're going to ruin my day?"

He winced. "I wish you hadn't put it that way. But yes, I have something I need to tell you."

"Go ahead. I don't think my brain can deal with waiting."

"I talked with Brandon this morning. We both agreed." He peered into her eyes. "We don't think the creep that Zoey texted with is the person who took the pictures."

Her stomach dropped. There was a second person trying to ruin her and Zoey's peaceful life? "Why do you think it's another person?"

His chest rose and fell. "A child predator focuses on the child. They don't change their preferences, and he wouldn't allow his attention to spillover to an adult."

"So, because I'm in some of the pictures, you've concluded that it isn't the same guy."

"Because you are the focus in those photos, yes."

She rubbed her temples. "I can't believe this is happening."

"I'm sorry, Jennie. I truly am."

"It's not enough that someone attempts to lure my daughter out to meet him through a mistaken text..." Her voice rose. "But now someone else is involved." Blood whooshed in her ears.

"Jennie."

"Don't Jennie me." She scanned the room and discovered several patrons staring at her. She lowered her voice. "What am I supposed to do? How am I going to protect my daughter?"

"Nothing is going to happen to Zoey. And I'm worried about you too. Brandon and I are going to work both angles until we find out who's responsible for the pictures and both attacks, the text message and the lake incident." He lifted his cup and took a sip. "That is a promise."

Jennie rested her head on the back of the bench seat. "Pinewood Shores was supposed to be safe. No one was supposed to find us here."

David's brows pinched together. "Find you?"

Tears welled in her eyes. Why had she said that? "Thanks for letting me join you for coffee and for the update, but I need to head out. Today's my day off, and I need to run errands and check on Tina before we join Zoey at Aunt Emily's."

His shoulders slumped. "I'll keep you posted. And Jennie?"

She peered at him.

"Stay safe."

She nodded and slid from the booth. Hitching her purse strap higher on her shoulder, she rushed out the door.

By four that afternoon, she had composed herself and found a new wave of determination.

Errands complete, she picked up Tina, and the two of them waltzed into Aunt Em's house.

The scent of cinnamon and sugar swirled in the air.

She closed her eyes and drew in a deep breath. The smell brought back wonderful memories of living with her aunt. The woman tended to bake for the entire town, or so it seemed.

How had she allowed her life to go so far off the rails before turning back to the woman who'd taken her in as a hard, saucy teen and loved Jennie until she'd softened. When she'd married Brad and moved away, she missed her connection with Aunt Em but was determined to make a new life with her husband and have the family she'd always dreamed of.

Brad hadn't been the man she'd thought he was, but she had committed to making the best of their marriage. Then he'd died and she became that lost teenager once again. Making stupid choices and being too afraid to stand on her own. Enter Kenny. A man who'd promised to help her and support her after Brad's death. Saying he owed it to his friend.

Little did she realize at the time that he'd laid the groundwork for her dependence. Small things like telling her she couldn't support herself and Zoey without help progressed to bigger things like she was too stupid to be a nurse. No woman worthy of being called mom would leave her child during the day and that her place was in the home. It hadn't been until Zoey turned three that Jennie found herself not only in Kenny's house but in his bed as well. Once he'd talked her into becoming *his girl* as he'd called it, Kenny had shifted from hurtful words to physical violence.

No one had noticed the bruises. Not even her friend Tina or Brad's friends, Levi and Adam. Kenny knew where to hit her that wouldn't be visible.

Her one and only friend, Tina, who lived down the street, had discovered the abuse a year later.

Tina had begged Jennie to get help, but she'd refused, taking the blame for Kenny's actions. It wasn't until Tina discovered her near death by the hands of Kenny that Jennie found the strength to face her mistakes and come home to her Aunt Emily's love.

She looked back now and wanted to scream at her weakness. And all the time wasted. She blinked away the horrible memories.

Laughter bubbled from the kitchen.

Jennie smiled. "Em? Zoey?"

"In here, honey."

"Come on, Tina. I want you to meet my Aunt Em." She followed the voices to the sunny room filled with pans of cinnamon rolls.

"Hi, Mom. Hi, Aunt Tina." Zoey grinned.

"Looks like you two have enough sweets to feed half the town of Pinewood Shores."

"I thought Pinewood Shores' finest needed a special treat for all their hard work finding the man who tried to hurt my precious girl." Aunt Emily ran a hand down Zoey's hair. "And my helper agreed."

Jennie introduced the two women and gave her aunt a quick rundown of her friendship with Tina.

Aunt Emily sniffed and wiped her eyes with her apron. "I don't know how to thank you."

The back door swung open interrupting the conversation and a familiar figure stepped through the entry. Jennie's breath caught in her throat.

David stomped his feet on the mat. "All done, Miss Emily. Anything else I—" His eyes widened. "Jennie."

"Hi, David. I see someone"—she pinned a glare on her aunt—"has you working during your off hours."

"Not exactly." His sheepish grin reminded her of a guilty little boy. "I'm not off duty. But Miss Emily needed help, so I called out of service for a few minutes to assist a damsel in distress." He kissed Aunt Em's cheek.

The older woman patted his face and mock huffed. "I'm not helpless, but it sure is nice to have a big strong man help."

Jennie wasn't sure if she wanted to laugh or groan. "Aunt Em."

David chuckled. "Always at your service, ma'am." He reached to snag a roll.

Aunt Emily swatted his hand. "Wait a minute and I'll box a couple dozen for you to share with the boys downtown."

"Are you kidding? If I leave here without goodies, I'm a dead man." He quirked a smile then went to the sink and washed his hands. "Nice to see you again, Tina."

"Likewise." Tina pursed her lips fighting the smile trying to escape.

Emily handed David two boxes of cinnamon rolls a few minutes later. "Jennie, be a dear and help this young man to the door." She raised a frosting-coated hand. "I'm a bit too messy to escort him out." The woman grinned and winked at Tina.

Oh brother. Could her Aunt Em be any more obvious?

She walked David to his car parked across the street. "Sorry about that. Aunt Emily is not known for her subtlety."

"She's a great lady. I'm honored to be asked to assist her with tasks around the house."

"I'm grateful for your willingness. She's a gem. I wish I wouldn't have stayed away as long as I did."

He dipped his head and peered into her eyes. "I'm glad you decided to come back."

David made it sound as if she'd chosen to be away too long and came home out of loneliness. But the truth? She'd feared for her life and needed to feel the love of her Aunt Emily again. "I am too."

He rested his hand on her shoulder. "Please thank Miss Emily again for the cinnamon rolls. The boys will love the treat."

"I will. And David"—she covered his hand with hers—"stay safe out there."

He smiled and slid into the driver's seat. Hand on the door handle, he paused. "See ya later, Jennie." And with that, he pulled the door closed, started the engine, and drove away.

She watched his vehicle disappear around the corner. If she had the luxury of having a normal relationship, David would be at the top of her list. But that was out of the question. It would require her to spill her secrets, and she had no intention of doing that.

CHAPTER 9

Monday 2:30 p.m.

Cinnamon rolls in hand, David entered the station. His mind on Miss Emily's matchmaking attempts. He wasn't opposed to asking Jennie out, but the secrets she held concerned him. He hoped he'd gain her trust before something terrible happened to her or Zoey. The alternative—another death on his conscious—would have irreversible consequences to his heart.

"Is that a Miss Emily box?" Officer Carlson stepped beside him. A hopeful look plastered on his face.

"Sure is." He lifted the lid, plucked out a couple rolls, and handed the box to the young officer. "Here. Put that in the break room and spread the word."

Carlson scurried away with the treasured treat.

David meandered through the office maze and sat on the corner of Brandon's desk. He handed his partner one of the cinnamon rolls. "Looks like you could use a pick me up."

Brandon leaned back in his chair and released a contented sigh. "Absolutely."

"How's the research coming along?" David asked between bites.

"Not too bad. I've found evidence against Eddie Winters while waiting for our search warrant. I think we have our guy."

"Good." David licked his fingers. "How much longer before we get the go ahead?"

"Shouldn't be too long. I'm expecting the paperwork by the end of the day. We'll be ready to go tomorrow."

"I don't care if it's earlier in the week than normal, I want this creep behind bars." David skirted Brandon's desk and plopped down at his own. He pulled out two handwipe packets he'd thrown in the top drawer from one of their food deliveries and tossed Brandon one.

Powering up his computer, he opened his email and closed his eyes. Sixty-two messages. He'd only been away from the station for an hour. He inhaled and got to work.

"Detective?"

David checked the clock at the bottom righthand corner of his computer screen. He hadn't looked up in over two hours. No wonder his eyes burned. He opened and closed his eyes a couple of times then lifted his gaze to the receptionist. "What can I do for you, Bethany?"

A pizza box in hand, she grinned at him. "Giving up and eating at work now?"

He scrunched his forehead. "Not that I know of."

"Well, the delivery guy said this was for you." She placed the box on his desk. "Enjoy."

He turned to his partner. "Brandon, you order pizza?"

"Nope. I plan to be home in time to eat with the kids tonight. You?" Brandon rolled his office chair next to him.

"Not me." David lifted the lid on this pizza box. He shoved his chair backward and leapt to his feet. "What in the world?"

A large supreme pizza with cockroaches sat before him.

"Interesting topping," Brandon deadpanned.

David rolled his eyes. "Thanks, partner." Inching his way to the nasty insect infested pizza, his gaze landed on the inside of the lid.

He stared at the message written in red block letters. *Stay away! She's Mine!*

Officer Hanes appeared at his side and slapped his back. "Who'd you make mad?"

He heard Brandon on the phone calling the county Crime Scene Unit to come collect his delivery as evidence.

"Not a clue." He peered at the creepy crawlies again and shivered. At least the disgusting bugs were dead.

"Well, someone doesn't like you." Hanes leaned in and examined the words.

Brandon hung up. "You go on a date with a wrong girl lately?"

"No." David glared at him. The man knew he'd only dated a few times since he'd arrived in Pinewood Shores. He hadn't forgiven himself for letting down Brenda. His lack of attentiveness had gotten her killed. If he'd only left work instead of letting his job come first. "As a rule, I don't date. You know that."

"Had to ask." Brandon pulled his cell phone from his belt clip and snapped a few pictures.

Hanes scooted a chair over and plopped down next to the detectives. "It has to be someone you're involved with."

David opened his mouth to respond, but the officer held up a hand to stop his rejection of the idea.

"Look, I'm not asking about women you have or haven't dated. I'm asking if there are any new ladies in your life, including cases or casual friendships."

He stared at a spot on the white colored wall on the other side of the room. Who had he met in the past few weeks? Only one name came to mind. "Jennie."

Brandon lowered his cell phone. "That doesn't make sense. Eddie's focused on Zoey, not Jennie. He wouldn't care what your relationship is with her mother. Unless..."

"Unless we're right and there's a second suspect unrelated to the internet crime against Zoey." He flinched. Maybe their earlier theory at the coffee shop hadn't been far off. But who? "Do you have any more info on Jennie's background?"

His partner shook his head. "Nothing. There's a glitch in the online system and I keep playing phone tag with the detective in Indiana. Since it was background only, I hadn't pushed to get the information."

"I'd say it's time for a hard shove." David ran a hand through his hair. Staring at the cockroaches, he cringed. Man, he hated those little critters. "We have to find out if she has any enemies."

The wheels of Brandon's chair squealed as he rolled behind his desk. "On it."

The CSU team arrived, and David gladly moved to an unoccupied desk.

Pinewood Shores might be small, but the police department shared a CSU unit with two other neighboring towns. Something he was extremely thankful for. He'd collected his own evidence in the past when needed but preferred to hand off the job to a team trained specifically for that task.

Brandon leaned his hip against the corner of David's borrowed desk. "Finally got a hold of the detective. He's pulling together the information I requested and promised to send it to me tomorrow morning."

David leaned back in his chair and clasped his hands behind his head. "Why not tonight?"

"Something about power outages due to a storm and everyone available is tasked with public safety. And for a bit of good news, the signed warrant for Winters is on its way."

"At least you connected with Indiana." David sat up. The back of the chair thunked to the upright position. "Let's focus on Eddie and then we can turn our attention to whoever doesn't like me."

His partner studied him for a long moment then nodded. "Just watch your back. Call me if you need help."

"Will do." He gathered his papers and stood. "I think I'll head home and get some rest before we serve the warrant tomorrow."

"Sounds like a plan." Brandon meandered to his desk and logged off his computer. "Take it easy, Whitman."

"You too, Pierce." He watched his partner say goodnight to Bethany and push through the double doors at the entrance.

David rubbed his eyes with his thumb and forefinger. His shoulders slumped. Questions swirled in his mind. Who hated him? What had he done? He closed his eyes. The biggest question of all, would this be the case that cost him his life or the life of another?

***

Jennie held the mouthpiece of her phone over her head, kissed Zoey on the forehead, then shooed her off to bed while waiting for David to answer her call. Her friend Bethany, who worked for the police department as a receptionist, called her a few minutes ago about David's surprise delivery. The story had given Jennie the creeps. Unable to stop worrying, she gave in and dialed his number.

"Hello?" David's voice filtered over the phone line.

"Bethany told me what happened. Are you okay?"

"I assume you're talking about the Coach Roach pizza." His breath hissed across the connection.

"Yes." Jennie shivered. Creepy crawlies in or on her food would give her nightmares.

"I wasn't too fond of the topping that's for sure." He chuckled.

"It's just downright disgusting. Do you know who sent it?" She tugged the ponytail holder from her hair and ran her fingers through the strands.

"Not a clue. Someone ordered it online and sent it to the station. The pizza place claims it was purchased by James Smith."

"Who's James Smith?"

"Someone who doesn't want to be identified. Pick a common name and no one knows. Kinda like John Doe."

"I'm sorry that happened to you today." She clutched the phone to her ear and ambled to her bedroom. "Anything I can do to help?"

"Thanks, but I'm fine."

She paused at his hesitation. "You're sure?"

"Well..."

"Yes?"

"Maybe you could talk to me for a while. I'd really like that."

She smiled. "Tell ya what. Go do whatever you need to do. I'm going to change and brush my teeth. Then we can chat a little bit before we both need to get some sleep."

"Sounds good. I'll be back in a second." A clunk sounded on the phone. Most likely David placing the phone on a table.

Jennie tossed her phone on her bed. Grabbing her clothes, she rushed to the bathroom, changed, washed her face, and brushed her teeth. She took a deep relaxing breath. Flicking the light switch off, she padded into her bedroom.

She scooped up her cell. "Are you still there?"

"Yup." David mumbled and paused. "Sorry for chewing in your ear, I grabbed a sandwich."

"Hope it came without the insects this time," she razzed him.

"Not funny. That thing was disgusting." He tossed back, taking the joke as she'd intended.

"I'll let Aunt Emily know you'd love cookies with extra protein next time."

He groaned. "Oh stop. That's just gross. I'm trying to eat here."

"I'll quit. But it's so much fun to tease you." Not in a thousand years would she have ever dreamed of enjoying a man's company. But she was coming to like and trust the kind detective on the other end of the phone.

"Okay, so if insects are off the table." She cringed. "Sorry. Bad pun."

"You're killing me here."

She laughed. "What I was trying to ask...besides the icky delivery, how was your day?"

"Same old, same old. Working on warrants, contacting creeps, you know, all the glorious police work."

"Sounds like fun." She curled into bed and rested against the headboard. "Well, I hope nothing exciting happens tomorrow."

"In police work, boring is good."

She bit her lip. She needed to apologize to the man for Emily's attempt at bringing them together. "Listen, I'm really sorry for..." Prickles skittered up the back of her neck. She straightened and scanned the room.

"Jennie? Jennie, what's wrong?"

"I-I...um...something's off." Her gaze shifted to the window. The closed blinds gave her a bit of comfort, but she couldn't shake the feeling of being watched.

"Where are Tina and Zoey?"

"Tina went home today, and Zoey's in bed."

Keys jingled through the phone line. "Keep talking. I'm on my way."

"No, I'm fine. Just an odd sensation."

"Are you sure?" The man didn't sound convinced.

"Positive. I'm just tired." She slid down beneath the comforter and pulled it to her chin. As if the cloth would protect her. She shook her head at the ridiculous thought. "Tell me something funny to get my mind off of the weird happenings from the past few days."

David sighed. "As long as you promise to call day or night if you need help."

The knot in her stomach loosened. "I will."

"Thank you. Now, let's see. Did you ever hear about the time Brandon tried to arrest a raccoon?"

"No, I don't think I've heard that one." She appreciated him attempting to distract her.

Thirty minutes later, Jennie disconnected the call and placed her phone on the nightstand. David's voice had eased her panic, but now that he wasn't in her ear, the sense of dread fell over her like a cloak. The sensation of being watched returned. Her throat tightened and her pulse raced. She gulped for air.

Clutching her blanket to her chin, she visually searched the room.

Nothing out of place. She had to get a grip. But what had triggered her panic?

CHAPTER 10

Tuesday 1:00 p.m.

The odd pizza delivery yesterday and Jennie's anxiety last night had him mulling over reasons for both. As hard as he tried, nothing seemed to take hold as an answer. A slap on the back from his partner shifted David's thoughts to the task at hand—serving a warrant to the creep who targeted Zoey.

He focused on the sidewalk edging the street. A couple ambled toward them laughing as their dog pranced around, getting tangled in its leash.

He clicked the mic on his shoulder. "Hanes. Take care of our visitors down the street."

"Ten-four, detective."

The search warrant came last night, and he and Brandon spent the morning strategizing and bringing the team up to date on the latest intel. With everyone in place, the last thing they needed was unwanted civilians in danger.

The weight of his Kevlar vest trapped the heat of the hot July sun. Sweat trickled down his back and dotted his forehead. He patted his tactical pants confirming his extra clip was in place.

He nudged his partner. "Ready?"

Brandon scanned the area and turned to face him. A look of boredom crossed his partner's face. "Yup. Let's go get the bad guy."

David pursed his lips to hide a smile. Leave it to Brandon to be relaxed about walking into a dangerous situation. He wished he had the same ability to compartmentalize, but past experience had taken that away.

Taking a deep breath, he released it through parted lips. His heartrate lowered. His hands grew steady. He was ready to take down the guy who'd brought fear into Zoey's life.

He engaged his mic. "Okay, boys and girls, stay alert." He nodded to the man with the battering ram to take his place at the bottom of the porch steps.

He and Brandon slipped in position on either side of the front door. He rolled his neck then pounded on the wooden frame. "Police! Search warrant! Open up!"

Silence met his command. No scuffling. Nothing. He narrowed a questioning gaze at Brandon.

His partner shrugged.

"Eddie Winters! Open up!"

Still nothing.

"All right, take it down."

Five seconds later, the door hung at an awkward angle and his team swarmed inside. Shouts of "Search warrant" echoed throughout the house.

"Whitman! I got a body."

The light smell of decomp met his nose. He wound his way to the back of the house and stepped into the kitchen.

Officer Carlson crouched just beyond the pool of blood under the lifeless form of Eddie Winters.

"Not how I wanted this to go down," he muttered.

Carlson raised an eyebrow. "Well, he made someone mad, and it wasn't us." The man pointed to Winters's face and torso. "Appears someone hated him. Looks as though whoever it was took their time beating him to a pulp before putting a bullet in his chest."

David rubbed the back of this neck. "Get the crime scene team here and figure out who did this." He spun and headed to find his partner.

"Here." Brandon handed him a stack of photos.

Blue gloves on, he accepted the offering and flipped through them. His stomach churned. "Winters was a class A..." No, he'd made a vow to clean up his language. But right now, he wished he hadn't. He exhaled. "This dude was sick."

He shoved the offending pics back at Brandon. "Take 'em. I'd rather not see those again. I need some air." He snapped the plastic gloves from his hands and stomped out the front door.

Arms folded across his chest, David leaned against his department vehicle. He watched as his team wrapped up their duties in silence and the M.E. shoved the gurney in the back of the van. He'd say "what a waste" but was it really? He closed his eyes. What kind of man thought that about another human? Every life had potential, but at the moment, he couldn't find it in Eddie's. The guy took the word disgusting to a whole new level.

For now, David would be satisfied that another pedophile was off the streets for good. Later, once the bile in the back of his throat subsided, he'd reconsider—maybe.

Brandon appeared seemingly from nowhere. A crease marred the man's forehead. "Let's go get the paperwork done."

He nodded and circled the car.

The events of the day had taken their toll on the team. The evidence found in the house had several officers including himself exiting the building for a bit of fresh air before returning to their duties.

Instead of forming a case against Eddie, he and Brandon now searched for the person who murdered their suspect.

Back at the station, David paced the bullpen.

Brandon pushed out a chair with his foot. "Sit. You're making me edgy."

He sat, then stood. "Sorry. I need to get out of here for a few minutes."

"Whitman."

He pivoted and caught his partner's questioning gaze.

"What's going on?" Brandon asked.

"Something's not sitting right, and I can't put my finger on it."

"I'm listening." Brandon leaned back in his office chair and clasped his fingers behind his head.

David ran a hand over his hair. "I don't know. That's what's driving me nuts." He stared at the wall behind his partner. "Look, I'm outta here for a few."

He all but ran from the station. Flipping open the Velcro pocket in his pantleg, he grabbed his truck keys. He slowed and lifted his face to the sun. What was wrong with him? He'd never left his partner hanging before.

The heat penetrated his tactical pants and department polo shirt and warmed his cheeks.

He glanced at his truck. The thing would be baking from sitting there all day. He might as well cool it down before he got in and burned his hands on the steering wheel.

Pushing the remote starter, the engine revved and the world exploded.

Oxygen rushed from his lungs. His body flew through the air and blistering heat followed.

The world turned dark gray, and silence descended.

"David."

A voice spoke from a deep tunnel.

"Come on partner, talk to me."

His eyes fluttered open and he came eye to eye with Brandon.

"Can you hear me?"

"Kinda. Speak up." David lifted his hand and brought it to his forehead.

"I'm practically yelling."

"Oh." Well, that wasn't good. He wanted to close his eyes and go to sleep, but his partner wouldn't stop yammering.

"Lie still. Your body took abuse from that explosion. Paramedics will be here soon."

"Explosion?"

Brandon glared at him. "Are you serious? Or are you being Mr. Funny Man?"

"What exploded?"

"Your truck, dude."

A groan rumbled from his chest. He'd just made the last payment. Good thing for insurance. But would it cover an explosion? A sudden spark of memory hit him. He'd used the remote starter an instant before he'd found himself flat on his back. He blinked. Why on Earth was he concerned with insurance when someone had tried to kill him?

"Brandon?"

"We're on it. You just take it easy. I want my partner back in working order and soon."

David's stomach twisted. Who wanted him dead?

***

The Emergency Department had finally emptied after a busy morning. The fact no one sat in the waiting room was a miracle. Jennie leaned her shoulder against the wall and closed her eyes. Except for the short time she'd chatted with David, she hadn't relaxed last night. The eerie sensation had never left, and she hadn't slept much, if at all.

"You don't look so good."

Jennie glanced over to discover Tammy's concerned gaze.

"Long night?" Her friend waggled her eyebrows.

"Not a chance." She didn't date, and Tammy knew it. Her coworker had never asked, but Jennie had a feeling the woman had the basic idea why. "I couldn't sleep."

"I'd imagine you haven't had a good night's rest since this thing with Zoey started."

No, she hadn't. But that wasn't the reason she'd watched the clock change every hour last night. She shivered.

"Since it's eased up, why don't we hit the report room and take a break."

Jennie plodded behind Tammy to the other side of the main desk and into the small area they used for shift reports and a makeshift breakroom. Due to the crazy schedule of the Emergency Department, the hospital administrator had splurged for a single cup coffee maker, a microwave, and a small refrigerator.

"Sit. I'll get you a cup of coffee. You look like you need it." Tammy shooed her toward a chair.

Jennie plopped onto the hard plastic seat. She rested her head on the wall behind her and closed her eyes. "Thanks. The stress is catching up with me."

A hand gripped her shoulder.

"Jennie?"

Her shoulder shook.

"Jennie?"

She pried her eyes open and blinked. "Tammy?"

"Yeah, it's me. You fell asleep the second you stopped talking." Tammy placed a warm mug in her hand.

She inhaled the bold aroma. "How long?"

"I let you rest for ten minutes, then decided I'd better wake you up in case we get swamped by patients." Tammy took the seat next to her.

Jennie took a sip, then massaged the kink out of her neck. "I guess I needed it."

"I'd say. Want to tell me what's really going on?"

The ward clerk poked her head into the room. "We have an ambulance coming in from the police station. Something about an explosion."

"Who?" she demanded, but the petite woman had hurried off. Jennie's heart thundered against her breastbone. "It can't be him. It just can't be." She jumped from her seat and rushed to the emergency entrance.

Tammy stood next to her and rubbed circles on her back. "Want me to call for backup and you sit this one out?"

She shook her head. "No matter who it is, I have a job to do, and I'm going to do it." Inhaling, she planted herself at the door, looped her stethoscope around her neck, and gripped the ends.

Please don't let it be David.

The sliding doors whooshed open, and the hot July air slapped her in the face.

Mitch hurried next to the gurney, pushing it into the building. "Where do you want him, Jennie?"

Jennie focused on the older paramedic, afraid to find out the identity of his patient. "Bay one. We're clear right now. Vitals?"

Mitch rattled off the man's vitals, and she breathed a sigh of relief.

They worked in unison to transfer the patient to the ER bed.

The man groaned.

She unwrapped her stethoscope and prepared to use it. Steeling herself to look at her new patient's face, she swallowed. Her breath caught in her throat. She froze. Her fear had become reality.

David lay in front of her, IV in his arm, and an oxygen mask covering his nose and mouth.

A hand touched her forearm. "Jennie?" Tammy's whisper broke through her paralysis.

Jennie shook her head dislodging the cobwebs. *Treat him like any other patient.* She plastered a smile on her face and leaned over Detective Whitman. "I think Dr. Bennett was right. You can't seem to stay out of trouble."

Crinkle lines appeared at the corner of his eyes, indicating a smile, then disappeared.

Double checking his lungs and heart rate, Jennie opened the second drawer of the supply cart and removed plastic tubing. "Let's trade out the mask for a nasal cannula, then you can tell me what hurts."

David closed his eyes and relaxed his shoulders.

She exchanged the breathing devices. "David?"

He peered up at her.

"Here. Have some ice chips. Those oxygen masks tend to make your throat dry." She spooned a couple of tiny chips into his mouth.

He swallowed and whispered, "Thank you."

She nodded. "Now, tell me what hurts."

***

What hurts? Everything hurts. The more time that passed, the more he remembered and the more aches and pains he discovered.

He chuckled, then closed his eyes and groaned. "Remind me not to laugh."

"What's so funny?" Jennie placed her hand on his arm.

"Nothing. Absolutely nothing." His truck blew up, tossing him like a ragdoll, and the heat had licked his skin. The entire situation was a serious matter. But he couldn't help but chuckle at the insane idea that he could pinpoint his pain. He peered at her, taking in her narrowed gaze and the downturned corners of her mouth. "Sorry. I feel as though I've been in a fight with a professional boxer. At the moment, my entire body hurts."

She bit her lip. "Let's do some tests and get x-rays and a CT scan to see what's going on."

He rolled his head from side to side and regretted it as his head throbbed harder. "I know you have to do it, but just so you know, other than bruises and ringing in my ears, I'm okay."

"Really, doctor? You're sure of that?" Her hands fisted on her hips.

He cracked a smile. The woman was cute when she was grumpy. "The only thing I'm sure of is that I'm sore, but I don't think anything's broke."

"We meet again, eh detective." Dr. Bennett strolled up to his bedside.

"What can I say? I like your company." David rolled his eyes and grimaced. Even that hurt.

"Let's get those tests run that Jennie mentioned and get you set up in a room for the night."

David struggled to push himself up. "What?"

"Settle down, Whitman." Bennett eased him down. "I don't suspect anything serious by the way you're bantering with me, but I'm not jazzed about the story I heard of your flying through the air and losing consciousness. And the force of explosions can cause organ damage. I want to rule out any internal issues." The man patted his shoulder. "The stay overnight is only a precaution if the tests come back negative."

He took in the doctor's expression. Bennett wouldn't budge on this one. "If I have to stay, can we please keep this amongst ourselves for a while?"

"Too late." Bennett snorted. "I've already notified next of kin."

"You. Did. What?" He was going to kill the man with his bare hands.

"Calm down. Your parents were relieved to hear you're okay. Although, I expect they'll be here in..." The man checked his watch. "...a couple of hours. So, what do you say we get you out of here and settled before they descend?"

So much for staying under the radar and easing into the conversation with his parents. Especially his mom.

Dr. Bennett made notes on his chart and handed it to Jennie. "Take care of him. I'll check back in later."

Jennie nodded and straightened to her full height. "Detective, are you ready to get those tests started?"

"Um, yes?" He studied her. Why was she acting formal? His head pounded and his body felt like he'd been hit by a train. He didn't have the energy for games. "Look, I know something's wrong, but I don't know what I did to make you mad."

"Mad? You think I'm mad?" Her bottom lip quivered. "I'm trying not to fall apart." Moisture dotted the corner of her eyes. "I hear about an explosion and the next thing I know Mitch is rushing you into the ER. I'm not mad. You scared me to death." Her voice rose in pitch. "I have a job to do and worrying about you is making it difficult."

He clasped her fingers and rubbed his thumb along the back of her hand. "I'm okay, honey. I'm in one piece and I'll live. At least until my mother gets a hold of me," he muttered the last sentence.

"And I'm grateful, but my mind won't stop playing the 'what if' game." She tugged her hand away and held the edges of the stethoscope draped around her neck like her life depended on it. "You get your tests done, and I'll come find you later."

What choice did he have? "Promise?"

"I promise. I'll send Randy in to take you to x-ray, then go talk to your partner. I'm sure he's pacing a hole in the floor of the waiting room." She straightened his blanket and ran her finger across his hairline. "I'll see you later."

With that, she pivoted and strode out of his room.

He closed his eyes and exhaled. When had his heart betrayed him and fallen for the beautiful blonde who'd just walked out the door?

Three hours later, he laid his head against his pillow and closed his eyes. Thanks to Randy, he'd been able to take a short nap before his parents had received permission to enter his room twenty minutes ago and had fussed over him. But his energy had waned, and he didn't know how much longer he'd be able to stay awake.

Familiar lips kissed his forehead. "I'm just so glad you're okay." His mom's voice quivered.

"Give me a couple days and I'll be as good as new." He peered into the eyes of the woman who'd raised him and smiled.

"You better be, son." His dad patted his leg.

David grimaced, then recovered before his father saw. At least he hoped he'd covered the pain.

The door squeaked open.

Jennie took two steps in and froze. "I—uh—I didn't know you had company. I'll come back later." She spun to leave.

"Stop."

She paused and turned toward him.

"Please come in." He fumbled to find the bed controls to raise his head.

The bed rose, and he moaned at the movement.

Jennie rushed to him. "Hold on, tough guy." She adjusted his pillow and helped him move so the new position wouldn't hurt.

His breaths came quick and heavy. "Thanks."

"Sure." She started to back away.

He shot out his hand and grasped hers, stopping her retreat.

She stared at their hands then at him.

He cleared his throat. "I'd like you to meet my parents. Mom, Dad, this is Jennie."

***

Jennie lifted an eyebrow at David.

He wanted to introduce her to his parents?

"I'm Helen, this guy's mother. Thank you so much for taking care of him." His mother hugged her then handed her off to an older gentleman that was undeniably David's father.

The man held out his hand and she shook it. "Nice to meet you, Jennie. I'm James."

"It was wonderful meeting you, and I'm sure David would love to continue having you with him, but I need to check his injuries and confirm his next dosage of medication. I hate to do this, but I need you to step outside for a bit."

"No problem." James smiled at her. "He needs his rest anyway. We'll come back tomorrow to see how he's doing." David's father laced his fingers with Helen's, and the pair left the room.

David tipped his head back on his pillow and groaned. "I don't know how to thank you. I love them, but they can be a bit overwhelming at times."

Placing her fingers on the controls, she lowered his bed. "You looked ready for some peace and quiet."

David raised his arm and covered his eyes. "Who knew that mimicking a ragdoll shot from a cannon would hurt so much."

She paused adjusting his IV line. "David, you're lucky it didn't kill you."

"I know. I'm just grousing. Please, forgive me."

"Nothing to forgive. You're allowed." She grasped the fingers of his hand lying on the bed. "Get some sleep."

She started to step away, but his grip tightened, halting her motion.

"Jennie?"

"Yes."

"I know I don't have the right and you have a daughter waiting on you, but would stay with me for a while?"

How could she say no to this man? He'd been there for her ever since Zoey had called him.

"Of course." She scooted the easy chair next to his bed, never releasing her hold. "Get some rest."

A few minutes later, his breathing evened out and his hand went limp. She curled up in the chair and watched him for the next hour.

Her heart twisted when a nightmare struck, and David twitched and groaned.

She rose and smoothed her palm over his forehead. A tear slipped down her cheek.

"Who did this to you, tough guy?"

CHAPTER 11

Wednesday 11:00 a.m.

The aches and pains from yesterday were hitting a new high today. Stiffness had set in and moving was a new experience in pain. David rubbed the back of his neck wishing he could turn back the clock and start his truck while inside the station. He should be thankful he'd decided to cool down his vehicle before he got in it.

The hospital room door opened, and he glanced up to identify his visitor.

"Looking good for a man who got blown up yesterday." Brandon grinned.

"It'd be funny if it wasn't true." David waved the man toward the easy chair. "Have a seat and tell me you brought those files we discussed earlier this morning."

Brandon tapped the corner of the file with his palm. "Got 'em right here."

David adjusted his bed to a sitting position. His bruised body protested the new angle. "Never thought it'd hurt so bad to be thrown to the ground."

"You did hit the pavement pretty hard. You're fortunate there wasn't more damage to your head." His partner lowered himself onto the seat.

David couldn't argue with that. The phrase 'hit by a Mack truck' came to mind. He blew out a breath. "Let's see what you brought."

Brandon studied him for a moment then nodded. "Not all the results are in, but the preliminary findings show that Eddie Winters was murdered—"

"Well, duh. We knew that."

"Would you let me finish?"

"Go ahead."

"As I was saying, it appears that someone beat Eddie and then put a slug in the man's chest. What wasn't apparent during the walk thru was that the same someone must have been looking for something, 'cause Eddie's pictures, email, and website had been tampered with."

David stared at his partner. "You think this was about his crimes against children?"

"I do. But the question is who?" Brandon pinned him with a stare.

His muscles tensed. "It's not Jennie if that's what you're thinking."

"And why would I think that? First of all, Eddie might have invaded Zoey's privacy and tried to lure her in, but that's where it stopped. He never laid a hand on her. And second, if this was a woman, she had to be a body builder to leave his face in that bad of shape."

David rolled his shoulders. "Sorry. Guess I jumped to conclusions."

"No kidding. Now, let's talk about some serious suspects."

"Who do you have in mind?" David held out his hand for the report and Brandon obliged. He scanned the document.

"I have to confess, I was hoping you had an idea."

"Why on Earth would I have any ideas?"

"Because someone tried to kill you."

David's stomach dropped. "There is that."

"Besides, my gut says Eddie's murder is tied to your cockroach pizza and the bomb in your truck. By the way, Megan checked the department parking lot video, but whoever it was knew how to hide their actions. She has nothing." Brandon settled back in his chair.

Wonderful. No proof as to who put him in the hospital. David turned his partner's words about Eddie over and over in his head. "I still don't see a connection. Winters was a creep and hurt a lot of kids. We finally had the evidence to bring him down. How could that possibly be related to me?"

"Like I said, gut feeling. I have no proof or any reason to go in that direction, but with all my years of experience, something tells me it all ties together in a neat little package—scmehow."

"If you're right—and that's a big if—who would want Eddie and me dead, and more importantly, why?" David handed the paper back to Brandon.

"Don't know."

"Okay, forget about that for a second. What videos, files, pictures, etc. did the suspect mess with?"

"Still waiting on the lab, but I bribed Megan to give me her first impression."

"Oh, really." David grinned.

"Not a chance, man. I'm not interested. I've got teenage twins at home. You think I have time for a woman?" Brandon rolled his eyes.

David chuckled. "What did Megs say?"

"Said that it looked as though someone attempted to erase IP addresses of those who visited Eddie's webpage."

"Sounds like someone's paranoid." David rubbed his eyes and leaned his head against his pillow. They had a lot of nothing, and it was giving him a headache. But one thing still bothered him.

"Brandon?"

"Yeah?"

"What did I do to make someone want to kill me?" He sounded like a whiny child, but he didn't care. It was one thing to put your life on the line protecting the public, but to be targeted—that was a different story.

Brandon leaned forward and rested his forearms on his knees. "I have no idea, partner."

The door to his room swished open a foot. "May I come in?"

David's heart lightened at the sound of Jennie's voice. "Sure. Come join the party."

She slipped in and closed the door then turned and spotted Brandon. "Ah, so that's why there's a party in here."

Brandon snorted. "Yeah, that's me, Mr. Party Animal."

Jennie smirked then turned her attention to David. "And how are you today?"

"I'm fine." *Other than I hurt all over and my head feels like it will explode any minute, I'm great.*

Her hand fisted on her hips. "You do remember I'm a nurse and can see right through that macho act."

His shoulders drooped. He should have known he couldn't hide the truth from her. "Let's just say, I've been better."

"How's the head?"

"Like someone is hitting my brain with a hammer."

She nodded. "Thought so."

"Welp." Brandon slapped his knees and stood. "Since you're in good hands, I'll get out of here." He waltzed to the exit. "I'll check in on you later."

"Thanks, man. And watch your back."

"Will do." Brandon slipped from the room, leaving David alone with the pretty blue-eyed woman at his side.

"I didn't mean to run him off." She slid the chair closer and eased herself onto it.

"No worries. We were at a dead end anyway."

She nodded. "I talked with Dr. Bennett a few minutes ago. He said they were letting you loose in a few of hours."

"Hallelujah." David didn't want to spend another minute longer than he had to in the hospital.

"Not so fast there, tough guy. Doc said only if you had someone to stay with. He's not ready for you to be alone until the ringing in your ears stops. He's afraid you'll fall. He doesn't want to risk it."

David closed his eyes. Who could he stay with? His parents were out of the question. Besides, he'd insisted they head home earlier that morning. "I'll have to think on that."

"Afraid for your mom and dad?"

Wow, the woman was perceptive. "You could say that. Brandon and I were just talking about who might want to kill me."

Jennie's breath hissed.

"Sorry. I tend to be blunt. I—"

"No, it's okay. After everything that's happened, I can see your point."

"So, yeah, I'm not sure what I'll do. I might just have to stay here. It might be safer for everyone if I did."

She tapped her finger on her lips. "I have an idea."

He quirked a brow. What kind of crazy scheme was the woman plotting. "I'm listening."

"What about Aunt Emily?"

He jerked forward, regretting the movement. "Are you nuts?"

"Hear me out." She clasped his hand through the bedrails. "Aunt Em has a great security system. Not to mention she's only a few blocks from the police station. Plus, she likes you."

He took care when he shook his head. "I don't want her in danger."

"David, please think about it. She's feistier than she looks."

He laughed then grabbed his ribs and moaned. "You think your aunt looks mousey? Not a chance. That woman is a force to be reckoned with."

"So, you'll stay with her?"

He needed a place to stay if he wanted to get out of here, but with the town's favorite resident? If anything happened to the older woman, he'd have a death sentence for sure. He sighed. "Maybe. But only if she's aware of the dangers."

The smile on Jennie's face lit up the entire room. "Fantastic. I'll call her and let her know."

What had he done?

Not only was he a target, he'd just agreed to put Miss Emily's life in danger.

Father, forgive me.

***

Saturday 10:00 a.m.

After three full days at Miss Emily's, having his every want and need taken care of, including frequent visits with Jennie and Zoey, David stepped from Brandon's sedan and retrieved his overnight bag. He stared at his home. The place he'd bought when he moved to Pinewood Shores, forcing himself to put down roots—connect with the community. Becoming the man that he should have been all along. A man who put his friends and loved ones above his job.

"You sure you're good by yourself?" Brandon leaned across the console and peered at David.

"I'll be fine. I'm ready to be in my own bed. Besides, the injuries are dull aches now and my head has quit spinning."

"I'll let you get settled. Captain is having one of the patrol officers drop off your department vehicle until you get your truck replaced."

"Sounds like a plan. I'll see you at the station Monday morning?"

"Yes, sir. Wouldn't miss watching you on desk duty." Brandon laughed.

"Hey. You're my partner. Aren't you supposed to support me?" David quirked an eyebrow, but couldn't hide his grin.

"Not this time, man. This should be entertaining."

"You know I don't sit still well."

"That's why it'll be fun to witness."

David shook his head. He patted the hood of the car. "Go home and see your kids."

"Planning on it. And David."

"Yeah?"

"Be careful. We haven't found the guy who tried to blow you up."

"Will do."

Brandon pulled from the curb, and David turned and ambled up the sidewalk. He put the key into the lock and opened his front door.

Home, sweet home.

He scanned the quiet living room, a bit on edge. Nothing seemed out of place, but he couldn't shake the unease. He reached into the side table drawer and pulled out his off-duty Glock.

He had finished clearing the house when someone knocked. He went to the window next to the entry and split two blinds apart with his fingers. Officer Lauren Coleman stood on his front porch, keys in hand.

He opened the door.

"Detective Whitman, it's good to see you feeling better. Here are the keys to the black sedan in the drive. Captain said not to wreck it." Coleman chuckled.

"Cap thinks he's funny." David rolled his eyes. "Thanks for bringing it by."

"No problem, sir." She retreated down the steps ard climbed into a waiting squad car.

He dropped the keys on the side table and made his way to the kitchen.

He filled a glass of water and lowered himself onto a chair. Placing his weapon on the table, he stared at the metal object.

How had his life come to this? A target for some creep and checking his own house for an attacker.

CHAPTER 12

Sunday 7:30 p.m.

A quiet evening together, the cure for her and Zoey's stress. Curled up on the couch Jennie snuggled closer to her daughter. Despite all the unknowns that still lingered, a sense of peace descended. David was on the mend and the man responsible for targeting Zoey was dead.

She twirled her little girl's hair around her finger. It seemed like yesterday she had held Zoey in her arms for the first time. A bittersweet day. The moment she realized she was in the parenting world alone. But when the doctor had placed her beautiful girl in her arms, her fears vanished, at least temporarily.

The lights of the TV glowed on the walls, and the voices droned in the background.

Zoey's soft breathing indicated she'd fallen asleep.

Five years ago, Jennie had vowed to never put Zoey in harm's way again. Yet, here they were. Yes, the creep who'd tried to entice her daughter to meet him was dead, but the idea that the man had uploaded her baby's picture for other predators to view gave Jennie the willies.

What if Kenny had found the website?

She had to tell David about her past to keep her daughter safe. She should have told him days ago when this whole thing started, but she couldn't shake off the shame.

Growls and barks penetrated the quiet.

The hairs on the back of her neck prickled. Her neighbor's dogs, Max and Zeus, rarely made noise.

Heart racing, she lowered Zoey's head to the throw pillow and crept to the window. Spreading the blinds with her fingers, she peered out into the night. Max's teeth glinted in the moonlight while Zeus ran along the fence line.

Someone was out there.

Jennie gasped. She dropped her hand and flattened herself against the wall. Her mind raced with possibilities.

She hurried to the coffee table, snatched her cell, and punched in David's number. Cradling the phone against her ear, she paced the living room. Her gaze jerked to the front door. A rustle and light taps stole the air from her lungs.

"Whitman." His voice came through a tunnel on the other end.

"Help," Jennie cried, but her voice refused to work.

"Jennie? Are you there?"

She swallowed and pushed the words out. "Help. He's been here."

"Who? Jennie, what's going on?"

"The dogs. The front door." Her mind was a jumbled mess.

"I'm on my way. Stay inside."

Thank heavens he understood enough to know she needed him.

"Jennie? Did you hear me? Stay inside."

"Yes." She jostled the phone in her sweaty palm.

Zoey wiggled on the couch but remained asleep.

A few minutes later, a knock on the door echoed in the entry.

Jennie squeaked and slapped her hand across her heart. She peeked out the window. David was squatting on the porch studying something.

She flung the door open.

He stood and she threw herself into his arms. His hand rubbed up and down her back. "Shh. It's okay. I'm here now. I won't let anything happen to you."

Her body trembled in his hold. She had to get a grip on her emotions. She was stronger than this.

Determined to recapture the strength she'd fought so hard for, she shifted out of his embrace. "S-sorry. I shouldn't have fallen apart like that."

A glimmer of empathy shown behind David's gaze. "You know, it's okay to need help."

"True, but when you've had to be strong for so long, it's a tad difficult to let others in." She rubbed her arms as a chill passed over her.

"Well, you have help now. Miss Emily, Brandon...me."

"Thanks. I needed to hear that." She tossed a glance at the still sleeping Zoey. David was right. She had to let go of her fears and accept help for Zoey's sake. "What did you find?"

"Photos of you and Zoey taped to your door and all around your porch."

Jennie attempted to swallow past the Sahara Desert in her throat. "I thought the creep was dead."

"He is." David's jaw twitched. "This can't be him."

Her stomach churned. "Then who? Who would do this to us?"

"You tell me?" He clutched her shoulders and peered into her eyes. "Is there anyone who'd want to hurt you?"

Kenny. But it couldn't be him. He had no idea where she lived.

She shook her head.

David raised a brow.

"No one with the exception of Tina knows I live in Pinewood Shores. And I don't have any enemies here." She'd changed her phone number and hadn't left a forwarding address. No one from her past should know where to find her.

"All right, if you're sure." He pivoted and clasped the doorknob. "I'll take the pictures into evidence, then sweep the outside to make sure whoever it was is gone. Please promise you'll call if the dogs start barking again."

"Promise. And thank you." She closed the door behind him and rested her forehead against the wooden barrier. "Coward. You should've told him about Kenny," she muttered.

She returned to the living room, scooped Zoey into her arms, and headed down the hall. Bypassing her daughter's room, she laid the sweet little girl on her king size bed. Brushing a strand of hair from Zoey's forehead, Jennie placed a kiss on her daughter's cheek. "You're sleeping here tonight, princess."

Kenny's release from prison had rattled her. But how could it be him? Jennie rushed to check the window locks and closed the blinds as tight as possible. Running her fingers over the raised scar tissue on the back of her neck, she closed her eyes. She'd survived Kenny's beating only by the grace of God.

What if he was out there? And if so, would she survive again?

CHAPTER 13

M onday 10:30 a.m.

David had stayed awake half of the night worrying about Jennie. If he hadn't placed a call to dispatch at two in the morning and requested random drive-bys he wouldn't have slept at all.

"I don't understand who's doing this. Eddie Winters is dead. The threat should be over." David slid his chair away from his desk and ran his hand over the top of his head.

"I agree. This isn't about Winters anymore." Brandon tapped his pen on his notepad. "Jennie's not telling us something."

David sighed. "I know. I can't get her to open up. I hate to go behind her back to Miss Emily, but I might have to if this continues."

"Good luck with that. I've known Mrs. Hanover for years. She's not about to tell someone else's secrets, especially her niece's."

"Tell me something I don't know."

"Well, since you asked." His partner's grim look had David regretting he'd asked. "I heard back from the detective in Indiana."

"What did you find?"

Brandon scratched his jaw and opened a file folder. "You're not going to like it."

"Spill it, man. You're worrying me."

"And rightfully so. You know about her late husband, Brad's death, but what you don't know is that Jennie Nielson and her infant daughter lived in Indiana with Brad's friend Kenny. Five years ago, Kenny nearly beat Jennie to death. She was in the hospital for weeks recovering while her friend Tina took care of Zoey."

The breakfast he'd eaten earlier that morning threatened to come up. "Please tell me they arrested the man."

Brandon nodded. "He was sentenced to ten years in prison."

"Chump change for that crime."

"Agreed." Brandon tapped the report. "Once Jennie recovered, she came to live in her Aunt Emily's cottage. And the rest, as they say, is history."

David stood and paced in front of their work desks, ignoring his healing injuries. "Why didn't she say something?"

"My guess is she's embarrassed."

He spun to face Brandon. "Why on earth would she be embarrassed?"

"Because this wasn't the first time he'd laid hands on her."

Heat climbed David's neck. He wanted to punch something, or maybe a certain someone. Why hadn't Jennie left him before it happened? One day he'd ask, but not today.

Blowing out a long breath, David tamped down his frustration. "Can we confirm where this Kenny guy is?"

"Not yet. I just received the file about ten minutes ago. I haven't had a chance to do anything but read it " Brandon glanced at his watch. "I'll check into it once I finish my meeting with the captain."

He snatched his windbreaker. "I'm going to find Jennie. I want answers as to what happened to her. And I don't want to read it in a file." David made a beeline to his car but stopped short.

A lady and young girl exited the diner down the block.

He squinted then straightened. Jennie and Zoey. Perfect timing. He marched down the sidewalk, his temper and brain warring with each other. After listening to the details of Jennie's past, he had no doubt she had her reasons for not telling him. But how was he supposed to do his job if she kept things from him.

Cool down and hear her out. He could at least give her the opportunity to explain herself.

Jennie glanced in his direction and waved.

He raised his hand to return the gesture.

A man popped out from behind a green truck and slapped his hand over Jennie's mouth.

"Jennie! Zoey, run!" David pulled his weapon from his holster and sprinted toward the attack. "Police! Let her go!"

The assailant's gaze met his and in one swift motion, he threw Jennie to the ground and dashed around the corner of the building.

David skidded to a stop next to her and knelt beside her.

Jennie hadn't moved since the attacker tossed her aside.

"Jennie?" He brushed the hair from her face. Blood oozed from a cut on her temple. He yanked his cell phone from his pocket and called for an ambulance. "Hold on, honey. Help is on the way."

Small fingers rested on his shoulder. He shifted and peered up into Zoey's tear-filled blue eyes.

"Is Momma gonna be okay?"

"I don't know, Zoey. But I'm going to do everything I can to help her." Because if she didn't survive, another woman he cared about would die on his watch.

***

The cut on Jennie's temple throbbed in time with her heartbeat. She fingered the bandage and snuggled deeper into Aunt Emily's couch. Her body ached, but her heart was grateful. If David hadn't arrived when he had, she'd no doubt be dead. And what would have happened to Zoey?

"You doing okay?" David draped a blanket over her.

The material rubbed against the strawberry scrape that covered her leg. She sucked in a breath.

"Sorry." He attempted to adjust the cover and finally gave up. "Can I get you anything?"

"I'm fine, thanks to you." She snagged his hand and held it.

"Wish I had arrived a bit sooner. I hate that he roughed you up."

Jennie lowered her gaze. "I'm used to it," she mumbled.

The handsome detective tilted his head and studied her.

Why had she said that? She didn't want his pity. In fact, she'd rather not need him at all. Look where her desperation and dependence on a man got her last time. No, she appreciated David's help, but that's where it would end.

His mouth opened as if he planned to say something, then closed again.

Regretting her question before she asked, she continued anyway. "What's wrong? You look like a four-year-old that had his cookie stolen."

He sighed and ran his fingers through his hair. "Why didn't you tell me about what Kenny did to you?"

A whimper escaped her lips. "Who told you?"

"Brandon."

"How did he find out? No one around here knows except Aunt Emily and she wouldn't tell."

David paced the living room. "After we found the photos on your porch, he did a background check."

She struggled to sit up. "You had no right."

"I'm sorry, Jennie. I truly am. But if it helps us find who's doing this to you, it'll be worth it."

Her voice quivered. "I didn't want you to know."

Two strides and he knelt in front of her. "Why? I can't help you if I don't understand who might want to hurt you."

Her throat tightened. How would she face him now? "What did Brandon tell you?"

He shook his head. "No way. I want to hear it from you."

"You'll think I'm stupid."

He tucked a strand of hair behind her ear. "I promise you. I see you as smart, brave, and a survivor. Anything but stupid."

She stared into his eyes looking for honesty. She almost laughed. Being a good judge of character wasn't in her wheelhouse. She patted the cushion beside her.

David lowered himself next to her and took her hand in his. He didn't rush her. He just waited.

Taking a deep breath, she told him her pathetic story. "You know about my husband."

David nodded.

"Yes, Brad was an alcoholic, but for the record, he was a good husband. He loved me in his own way and helped me get my nursing degree. He just couldn't stay away from the bars." She picked at the edge of her blanket. "His friend, Kenny, had been hurt in the accident, so I stayed in his guest room and helped him while he healed. He was really nice to me at first. Even after I had Zoey, he was super patient with her." She smiled. "Infants aren't always easy to be around."

He returned her smile and squeezed her hand.

"One thing led to another, and he offered the comfort and love that I desperately needed at the time." A tear trickled down her cheek and she wiped it away. "I knew better than to live with a man I didn't love. Aunt Emily had brought me up right, but I was a new mother, alone in this world. I made choices that I regret to this day."

"Jennie. We all make choices we regret."

"Well, I made a doozy. You would think after Brad, I'd have been more careful." She kept her gaze on the coffee table. She couldn't bring herself to look him in the eye. "Anyway, it didn't take love for Kenny to entice me into his bedroom. I was desperate for a man to notice me—to take care of me."

"When did he start abusing you?"

She laughed, but there was no humor in it. "He treated me well for the first six months after I gave birth. Like a princess even. Brought me breakfast in bed on the weekends even.

Helped with Zoey. I thought. 'How can I be this lucky?' But it all changed, little by little."

David leaned over and grabbed a water bottle from the end table and handed it to her. "Here."

"Thanks." She unscrewed the top and took a sip. Placing the lid back on, she rolled the bottle between her palms. "At first it was verbal. Telling me how stupid I was and that no one would want me now that I didn't have the perfect pre-baby body. The dumb part was that I believed him. Words turned into shoves and then into fists. He'd never leave bruises where others could see. When we'd leave the house, we looked like the perfect couple."

David's jaw twitched. "How long did this go on?"

Jennie held the cold container against the road rash on her forearm. "Four years."

"Jennie..."

"Don't. I don't want your pity."

He clamped his lips shut.

"He finally beat me so bad I lost consciousness. Tina found me and called 911. I was taken to the hospital, she kept Zoey for me, and the police arrested Kenny. Once they discharged me from the hospital and I testified against Kenny, I packed up the little I had and came home to Aunt Emily."

David tucked a strand of hair behind her ear. His touch soft and tender. Unlike anything she'd ever experienced. "I wish you would have done that earlier."

She swallowed the lump of emotion in her throat. "Me too. But I can't go back now. I have to live with my mistake."

"I understand that." His faraway gaze spoke of a story he'd yet to share with her.

All the energy she'd stored up on her return from the hospital faded. "I'm sorry, David. But I need to go to bed. I'm fading fast."

"That's understandable. Let me help you to your room, then I'll ask Miss Emily where the bedding is for the couch."

She whipped her head around so fast the room spun. She gripped the back of the couch. "Excuse me?"

"After what happened today, I'm not leaving you or Zoey alone. I'm staying right here until this guy is caught."

All she could do is blink at him. He couldn't be serious.

***

David's proclamation had drained all the color from Jennie's face. He knew she'd fight for her independence. And after what she'd told him it hadn't shocked him. But if she thought he would leave her to fend for herself, she had another thing coming. He'd let down his fiancé and she'd died. Not going to happen with Jennie.

David clutched her elbow and guided her to her bedroom doorway. "Anything I can do for you before I go find Miss Emily?"

She bit her lower lip. No doubt holding back a protest. "No. I'm good. Thank you for all you've done today."

"I'd say it was my pleasure, but I never want to see you lying motionless on the ground again."

She touched the bandage on her temple and smirked. "Can't say I want to repeat the experience."

"I'll be in the living room if you need anything."

She nodded.

"Goodnight, Jennie." He turned and headed off to find Mrs. Hanover. They needed to have a discussion that was long overdue.

Emily stood at the kitchen sink scrubbing the bowl and utensils from baking cookies with Zoey earlier that evening. It seemed as though the woman loved to supply treats to everyone in town. Especially the police and fire departments.

He rapped on the molding framing the entryway.

The older woman pivoted. Spotting him, she grinned. "Come on in and have a seat." She wiped her wet hands on the apron tied around her waist. "I think I can rustle up some snickerdoodles and a glass of milk."

"That sounds amazing."

Plating four cookies and filling a glass, Miss Emily placed the treat in front of him.

"Thanks." He sank his teeth into the soft treat. "Mmmm. Only you can make them this good."

She laughed and patted his shoulder. Sliding out a chair, she plopped on it. "So, what can I do for you?"

He tilted his head and stared at her. "What do you mean?"

"Pardon my bluntness, but you look like someone dragged you through the woods and dumped you in the barn."

He threw his head back and laughed. "Where did you come up with that?"

She shrugged and grinned. "Something my mother-in-law used to say."

Sighing, he returned the cookie to his plate and dusted off his hands. "Miss Emily, why didn't you tell me about Kenny?"

Emily set her jaw. "It wasn't my story to tell."

"I needed to know."

"He's still in prison. If I thought he had anything to do with this, I'd have spilled the beans."

"Miss Emily, he's been released."

Wide eyes stared back at him. "Why would they let him out early?"

"According to the documents, they paroled him based on good behavior."

Tears pooled on her lashes. "That man almost killed her."

He covered the woman's hand with his. "Does he know where she lives?"

"The only person who knows is Tina, and that girl would give her life before she'd let Kenny know where Jennie went."

He made a mental note to find Kenny's whereabouts just in case he had discovered Jennie's location. "We'll do some more digging and see if we can find Kenny."

Emily patted his hand. "You're a good man, David. I'm sorry she didn't trust you enough to tell you before. But you have to understand, she's ashamed of her choices and for the longest time wouldn't show her face around town. She finally came around, and I gave her the keys to my cottage rental. Told her it was hers for as long as she needed it."

"When did she start working at the hospital? I've lived in Pinewood Shores for a few years now and haven't ever seen her."

"She got her Associate Degree in Nursing in Indiana before Brad died. During the time she hid out here, she took online classes and finished her bachelor's in nursing. It didn't take her long to finish. Soon after, she applied to the hospital. She worked on the medical floor for several years, then transferred to the Emergency Department about six months ago."

"Strange I've never seen her before. She still likes to stay in the background, doesn't she?"

"Of course. She has Zoey to protect."

"But Zoey isn't Kenny's child. Why would he want anything to do with her?"

"Because the man is insane. He thinks that Jennie is his property and that includes Zoey."

David rubbed the back of his neck. "Miss Emily, I don't have a good feeling about this."

Had Kenny somehow found Jennie and been behind her attempted abduction?

CHAPTER 14

Wednesday 7:30 a.m.

Two days later, David gritted his teeth. The stubborn woman claimed her injuries had healed enough and was determined to go to work today. Intending to keep his promise of supporting her, he opened the passenger door and helped Jennie into his department-issued vehicle. He'd drop Zoey off at school and Jennie at the hospital.

He slid into the driver's seat. "Oh, I almost forgot." He handed Zoey a brand-new cell phone. "Since your phone is monitored, the guys pitched in and got you a new one with a new number. I've added your contacts too."

Zoey squealed from the backseat. "Awesome! Thank you so much!"

"You're welcome, munchkin."

Jennie's jaw dropped. "You didn't need to do that."

"I know. But she needs to be able to have private conversations with you without the department reading everything you talk about."

He shifted to face Zoey. "I've added my number and Brandon's to your contact list. Please don't hesitate to call us if you need to."

Zoey nodded and smiled while she explored her new device.

"That's really sweet." Jennie's eyes filled with tears. "Please thank everyone for us."

"Will do." He gave Jennie Zoey's new number, and she added it to her phone. "Now, how about getting you ladies to school and work?" He turned the key and pulled away from the house.

After depositing Zoey at school, he drove to the hospital. "Are you sure you're ready for this?"

"Of course I am. It's only a few scrapes and a few stitches. I'm perfectly capable of doing my job."

"I know you're capable..." He clamped his mouth shut. No need to make the woman mad. He parked in front of the hospital's employee entrance. "I'll pick you up after work. Have a good day, and if you need anything, call."

"I will. Thanks." She stepped from the car, closed the door, and waved.

David's stomach churned as he watched Jennie walk up the sidewalk and disappear into the building.

Why had a storm cloud of dread suddenly surrounded him?

***

The familiar Iodoform odor tickled Jennie's nose. How a disinfectant smell could be so soothing, she'd never know. Running a hand over her blue scrubs, she checked in and joined her fellow coworkers for their informational meeting before starting her shift.

"Feeling okay, Jennie?" Tiffany rested her hand on Jennie's shoulder.

"Been better, but I'm good."

"Good. I hated hearing what had happened to you." Tiffany leaned in. "Did they catch the guy?"

Jennie sighed. "Not yet."

"I hope they do soon."

"Me too."

A request for help came from the ward clerk so she and Tiff veered to the left and headed for bay two.

Five hours later, Jennie finally had the opportunity to grab a bite to eat. She slipped into the staff room to retrieve her wallet.

Hands wrapped around her throat and squeezed.

She gasped for air, but none came. Clawing at the man's fingers, she wiggled and fought to get away. The hot rancid breath on her cheek made her gag.

"Stop fighting me. You know you deserve this." Her attacker tightened his grip even more.

Spots flickered on the edge of her vision. If she didn't do something soon, she'd be dead and no one would know until her coworkers found her body later in the day. She summoned her last bit of strength and kicked out connecting with a metal shelf.

The metal slammed against the table and chairs crashed to the floor.

The door squeaked open.

"What's going on?" Dr. Bennett's voice boomed in the small room.

Her attacker released his grip, and her body dropped to the tile.

Something smashed into the wall and the door slammed shut.

Her eyes refused to cooperate. Would her attacker come back and finish the job?

"Jennie?"

The deep male voice sounded through her tunnel of thoughts.

She had to get up.

She tucked her arms beneath her torso and pushed.

Falling back to the floor, the last thing she heard was Dr. Bennett yelling for security and a gurney.

***

David slipped into the driver's seat of the sun-warmed car parked in front of the home of the latest child they'd rescued. Sweat trickled down his back while his stomach threatened to revolt. How could people be so evil.

He stared out the windshield. "At least he's alive."

"Yeah. Too bad we didn't find him sooner." Brandon rubbed his temples with his index finger and thumb.

"It makes me sick to think what happened to that child. But the father is going away for a long time and the little boy is being placed in his grandmother's custody."

"He'll need counseling." David slid on his aviator sunglasses.

"Don't they all?" His partner slouched in the passenger seat. "I just keep thinking about my own kids. I don't know how I'd handle it if something so horrible happened to them."

"That's why we do this, man." He rolled his neck.

Brandon grunted.

"I'll admit, I'll be seeing that four-year-old in my sleep for quite some time."

"You and me both, brother."

David's radio crackled. "Unit 5, dispatch. Code 12-16"

David sighed. Great. An accident. "10-4."

Three minutes later, David pulled up to the accident scene and stepped out of his vehicle.

A petite elderly woman stood next to her car wringing her hands. "Officer. I'm so glad you're here."

"Detective David Whitman, ma'am." He held out his hand and she placed her delicate fingers into his. "Could you tell me what happened?"

The hipster thirtysomething man barged over. "I'll tell you what happened. She wasn't paying attention and plowed into me."

"Excuse me, sir, but I was asking the lady." The lack of manners, not to mention the guy's attitude, put David on edge.

"Fine. You want to listen to her drivel go right ahead. But I'm late for a meeting. You need to take care of this quickly."

The muscles in David's back and neck tightened. He clenched his fist. The guy was a jerk. "Listen here, buddy!" David seethed.

Brandon rested a hand on his shoulder, stopping him from saying something that might get him in trouble. He'd have to remember to thank his partner later.

The guy mouthing off might be a jerk but had no way of knowing he'd just left a scene where a four-year-old's father had done unspeakable things to the boy. One of the many things he wished people understood about his job. It might be a horrible moment in other people's days, but often times he'd seen things ten times worse before responding to the accident.

He inhaled and said a quick prayer for patience and proceeded to take care of business.

Accident taken care of, David slipped back into his car.

"Well, he was a nice guy." Brandon rolled his eyes and closed his door.

"A real peach." He started the car and headed toward the station. "Time to take care of the paperwork. I have to pick up Jennie soon."

"It's nice you're taking such an interest in her."

David glanced at his partner. The man's smirk lit up his face. "What's that supposed to mean? The woman's in danger. Am I just supposed to ignore her?"

Brandon chuckled. "No. But you're going above and beyond the call."

David gripped the steering wheel tighter.

"Relax. I think it's nice you've taken an interest in a woman. Thought maybe your fiancé's death had soured you for good."

Whether David wanted to admit it or not, the man had a point. He liked Jennie a lot. It wasn't as if he'd sworn off women. He just wasn't sure he was competent enough to take care of one he loved.

"Okay. Okay. I admit it. I like her," he grumbled.

"Now see, was that so hard?"

"You're a pain you know that?"

"What are partners for?" Brandon chuckled.

"Unit 5, dispatch."

Brandon picked up the mic. "Unit 5, go ahead, dispatch."

"Tell Detective Whitman to head to the hospital."

David flipped a U-turn. Gritting his teeth, he threw a glance at his partner. "Why?"

"Mind telling us why, dispatch?"

"There's been another attempt on Jennie Nielson's life."

David flipped on the lights and siren and sped through town.

"Copy that. ETA..." Brandon glanced at the speedometer, "three minutes."

"Or less if I can help it."

Horns blared as he barreled through the intersection two blocks from the hospital.

Brandon braced a hand on the roof of the car. "I'd like to get there in one piece."

"And I want Jennie safe. Guess we both might be disappointed."

He jerked the wheel and pulled up next to the Emergency Room entrance. He slammed the car into Park, jumped out, and rushed through the door, with Brandon on his heels.

Skidding to a stop at the intake desk, he leaned over it and got in the ward clerk's face. "Jennie Nielson. Where is she?"

"Calm down, Whitman." Brandon stood beside him, hands on the counter.

"Where is she?" His face heated and pulse skyrocketed.

"Detective. Take a breath." The clerk glared at him.

He squinted and caught a glimpse of the woman's nametag. "Look, Sheila. I need you to answer my question. Where is Jennie Nielson?"

The slide of a curtain and a deep voice captured David's attention.

"Whitman, would you relax. Ms. Nielson is going to be fine." Dr. Bennett's words almost took David to his knees.

"She's alive? She's okay?"

"Yes, but okay is a relative term. She's going to be sore and hoarse for a while. And I'm sorry to say she pulled her stitches out, so we had to fix that, but all in all, she's fine."

David swallowed past the lump in his throat and took a few steps toward the doctor. "May I see her?"

"Of course. But David…"

He stopped and stared at Bennett.

"Get it together before you go in there. She doesn't need you wigging out." The man clutched his bicep. "The bruises on her throat are not a pretty sight. So, hold it together. Don't react. She's a strong lady, but she needs your strength right now."

David nodded and slid the curtain aside.

Jennie lay on the bed. Her face pale against the purple and red marks on her neck. If the doctor hadn't told him otherwise, he'd have thought she was dead.

He entwined his fingers with hers. "Jennie? Honey, can you wake up for me?"

Her eyelids fluttered open. "David," she croaked.

"Don't talk. I just needed to see those pretty blue eyes." He brushed the hair from her forehead.

She smiled, then grimaced.

"What can I do for you?"

The look of pain tore a hole in his heart. He should have been here and kept her safe.

"You can stop blaming yourself," she whispered.

His heartbeat thundered in his chest. He'd only known her a short time and she had him pegged.

She reached for her water cup.

"Here, let me." He held the cup and straw for her while she took a sip.

Her eyes filled with tears.

He set the water back on the roller table and wiped her tears away with his thumb. "I know it hurts, and I'm so sorry."

"Not your fault."

"I don't want to make you talk, but are you up to telling me what happened?" He had to get her statement.

She laid her fingers across her neck and nodded. "As long as I can whisper."

"You can do anything you want."

She chuckled, then groaned.

He glanced over his shoulder.

Brandon stood at the opening, pen and tablet in hand, ready to listen to her account of the attack.

He'd have to thank his partner for the backup later. If his swirling thoughts of anger weren't enough to tell him he'd miss pertinent information, the pain in his heart would solidify the concept.

He gazed into Jennie's eyes. "Whenever you're ready."

Jennie spent the next five minutes going over every detail she could remember. The fact she understood that they needed anything and everything she could think of didn't get past David. Because of Kenny, the woman knew to remember details.

When she finished, he cupped her cheek with his palm. "You did good."

Her eyelids drifted closed, then opened again. "Sorry. I'm fading on you."

"Go right ahead and sleep."

"Will you be here when I wake up?"

"That's the plan. I need to talk with Dr. Bennett, but I'll be back."

"Promise?"

"Promise." He sucked in a breath as he watched the woman he was falling in love with.

Her eyes closed and her breaths became even.

He squeezed her hand, not wanting to let go.

Brandon cleared his throat. "Let's go interview the doc so you can get back in here."

David slipped his hand from hers and followed his partner down the hall.

He stopped in front of Dr. Bennett. "I can't thank you enough for saving Jennie's life."

"Honestly, detective, it was pure luck or divine intervention. Something. If I hadn't decided to grab my wallet from my locker when I did, I truly believe she wouldn't have made it."

The truth hit David like a sledgehammer. Jennie had come far closer to losing her life than he'd imagined.

What if the attacker succeeded next time? And he had no doubt there'd be a next time.

CHAPTER 15

Thursday 11:00 a.m.

Jennie's throat continued to burn as David assisted her into the truck he'd purchased earlier that morning. She inhaled the leather scent, wondering why new vehicles all smelled similar. Funny where her mind took her. Anything but dwelling on what had happened yesterday. Her breath caught. What if the man had succeeded in killing her? Zoey would be parentless. Yes, she'd have Aunt Emily, but as much as the little girl loved her great aunt, it wouldn't be the same.

A hand rested on her arm. "You doing okay?" Concern laced David's features.

She nodded.

"Are you sure you're ready to go to Miss Emily's?"

"I'd rather go home, but I don't think anyone will let me," she croaked. Great. She sounded like a frog.

"You have that right. The guys at the station plan to take turns patrolling your aunt's place."

All these years, she'd made friends but had never anticipated the lengths they'd go to keep her safe. "Please tell them thank you for me."

"Will do." He pulled from the parking lot, turned the corner, and headed up town.

They rode in silence for the ten-minute drive. She peered out the window and watched buildings and houses go by. She'd come to love this town. It was small, but not too small. It had allowed her the chance to disappear from society and then make friends when she came out of hiding.

Aunt Emily's house appeared, and Zoey stood on the front porch waving.

Jennie smiled. Her baby was safe. She couldn't wait to wrap her arms around her child and thank God for the opportunity to continue to raise her. Zoey had been her motivating force to finally leave a bad situation. Well, that and the near-death experience. Her stomach roiled at the thought of what Kenny might have done to her daughter if Jennie hadn't pressed charges.

For a moment, she realized what a blessing that final abuse had been. It got her off the fence. She'd rediscovered her stubborn independent streak she'd been known for...until Kenny.

"I think someone is ready to see her momma." David's low timbre pulled her out of her musing.

"I'm ready to see her too." She touched the marks on her neck. The visible fingerprints still startled her when she looked in the mirror.

His hand rested on her arm. "I've warned her. And don't forget, she came to your room while you were asleep. She knows. We've talked about it. Everything will be fine."

She stared into his chocolate eyes. She could get used to him taking care of her. But that was the problem, right? She'd done that once before and look where it had gotten her. Broken bones, scars, and a fear of being found. As much as she liked David, could she depend on him? Her heart said yes, but her mind—not so easy to convince. Deep down she knew he was nothing like Kenny. But letting go of her fears and relying on him...

"No child should have to see strangulation marks on her mother's neck. It's not right."

He squeezed her arm in comfort. "I agree, but there's nothing you can do about that. I think she just wants to make sure you're okay. Go give her a hug and snuggle with her a while."

The man was right. Zoey needed the assurance that her mother would be okay.

The corner of her lip curved upward. "When did you get so smart?"

He laughed. "I'm far from it, but it's what I would want if I were Zoey." He jumped from the truck and rushed to the passenger's side. Opening the door, he offered his hand.

She slid hers into his and cautiously stepped onto the sidewalk. She sucked in a harsh breath. Her body ached from the constant abuse over the last few days.

She peered up the walkway. Wow, it looked like a long trek.

David must have sensed her concern. "I've got you." He tucked her hand in the crook of his elbow and escorted her to the porch.

She hated being dependent, but she leaned into his strength anyway.

"Momma!" Zoey rushed down the two steps and threw her arms around Jennie's waist.

David released her and she ran her hand over Zoey's hair. "Hi, baby. How's my girl?"

"I missed you." Zoey's bright blue eyes stared up at her. "Are you okay?"

"I'm fine, pumpkin."

Her daughter's hands fisted and went to her hips. "Momma, don't lie to me. We promised. Remember?"

She had to smile. Zoey had made her pinkie swear a couple of years ago that they wouldn't keep secrets from each other. Her heart dropped to her toes. Her poor child had had to grow up so fast because of Jennie's mistakes.

"Momma?" Zoey glared at her.

"I remember."

"Well?"

Jennie sighed and gave up. Her daughter wouldn't be fooled. "I'm sore and tired, but I'm alive and back with my biggest treasure in the world."

Zoey studied her then gave a nod of approval. "I believe you. Aunt Em and I made potato soup. Your favorite."

"Sounds wonderful. Lead the way." Jennie smiled. Out of all her mistakes and bad choices, Zoey was the shining spot of her life.

David leaned in and whispered, "She's a little firecracker."

Jennie laughed. "You have no idea."

"Just like her momma."

Most women would be furious at being called a firecracker, but not Jennie. David's words were a balm to her battered heart.

After a bowl of soup, and snuggling with her daughter on the couch, Jennie's eyes drooped. Exhaustion took over and she couldn't stop it.

"I'm sorry, guys, but I'm tired." She stood and wobbled. David's hands shot out and steadied her. She smiled her thanks and headed toward the hallway. "Please don't let me sleep too long."

"You need your rest." Aunt Emily rested her knitting in her lap. "But I promise to wake you for dinner."

Jennie closed the door to her bedroom and released a long breath. She slipped into an oversized t-shirt and yoga pants. Her bedroom window caught her attention. She padded across the floor in her bare feet and peered through the partially closed blinds.

Hair stood up on the back of her neck. Was her attacker out there? Or was she paranoid? Heart racing, she tightened the blinds and tugged the curtain closed.

"Calm down. He's not looking in your window." The attempt to convince herself failed, but tiredness had taken over. She slipped beneath the covers of her bed. What if she was wrong and the assailant was out there?

Tears dripped across her nose and onto her pillow. Would she ever feel safe again?

***

The next morning, David folded the blanket and placed it on the corner of the couch. The bold aroma of coffee drifted into the living room begging him to get a cup of the mind-clearing substance. He stepped into the kitchen and discovered Zoey and Miss Emily working side by side at the counter.

"Hello, ladies." He made his way to the coffee pot and poured a cup. Leaning against the counter, he crossed his ankles and took a sip. His eyes closed as the flavor and warmth teased his taste buds.

"Hi, Mr. David. Aunt Em and I made Momma her favorite chocolate chip muffins. Want one?"

"Do I ever. You two are wonderful cooks." He accepted the plate with two muffins and sat at the kitchen table. "Don't you have school today, Zoey?"

"Yup, but I'm ready. Just need to eat breakfast." The girl grinned and plopped down in the seat next to him.

David glanced at his watch. He needed to run home, change, and get to the station, but he'd make sure Zoey got to school before he took care of his schedule. "Eat. Then I'll drop you off on my way to work."

"Okay." Zoey stuffed a huge piece into her mouth and chewed.

Jennie meandered into the kitchen. "That smells amazing."

David took a long, hard look at Jennie. Her pale face, a stark contrast from the deepening purple and black bruises on her neck, made his teeth clench. If he ever got his hands on the man who did this...

"How are you this morning?"

Jennie's gaze darted to Zoey.

The young girl raised a brow as if to challenge her mother to speak the truth.

"I'm sore, having bad dreams, and paranoid someone is watching me." She returned a raised brow back at Zoey.

The girl nodded and continued to eat her muffins.

He chuckled. The two were an interesting pair. Mother and daughter in every way, but also best friends and confidantes. He admired Jennie for not sugarcoating things with her daughter. The ten-year-old seemed wise beyond her years, but that hadn't stopped her from being a normal kid either.

"How 'bout I take Zoey to school, then come back during my lunch break and see how you're doing?"

"Sounds nice, but you don't need to. I'm sure you have a million other things that need to be done. And I assume I'll have a babysitter outside most of the day."

"You assume correctly. But that won't stop me from checking on you." He smiled and scooted his chair back. "Ready, Zoey?"

"Yup. Give me two minutes to brush my teeth." The girl placed her dish in the sink and raced to the bathroom.

David ran a hand down Jennie's arm. "Take it easy today. Promise me you'll rest and not go out of the house."

Pink rushed up her cheeks. "I promise."

He studied her a moment. That seemed too easy for the independent, stubborn woman he'd come to know. As he was about to ask her about the change in attitude, Zoey came screeching to a halt beside him.

"I'm ready." Backpack over her shoulder, Zoey took his hand and yanked him toward the front door. "Come on. I can't be late."

He chuckled and threw a smile over his shoulder at Jennie then turned his attention on Zoey. "You chariot awaits, princess."

Zoey giggled. "Can we run the lights and sirens?"

"I don't think so."

The corners of her mouth drooped.

"Maybe we can hit the lights once when we get to the school."

"Yay!"

CHAPTER 16

F riday 1:00 p.m.

What a day. He and Brandon reported to a domestic disturbance. His second-most hated call behind anything that dealt with children. The resulting release of the husband continued to baffle him. How did a woman put up with being hit and then scream at them not to arrest her husband? Now, he was late for lunch with Jennie. David pulled up to the curb in front of Mrs. Hanover's house and killed the engine.

He dropped from his new truck and waltzed over to Officer Hanes's car.

"Has it been quiet around here?"

Randy dusted crumbs off his shirt and peered up at David with a sheepish grin. "Yes, sir."

David swiped his hand over his mouth to hide a smirk. "Miss Emily makes amazing cookies, doesn't she?"

The officer exhaled. "She sure does."

"Relax, Randy. No one's going to grump at you."

"Thanks, detective. I had to use the facilities, and Mrs. Hanover handed me a bag of treats on the way out."

David nodded. "I get it. No worries, man. I'll be here for about an hour or so. Take a break and get some real food in your belly."

"Will do. See you in an hour, sir."

David waved at the officer as he backed out of the driveway. The weight of the day draped over his shoulders like a blanket. He clomped up the steps and knocked on the front door.

Miss Emily swung the door open and greeted him with a hug. "You're a sight for sore eyes."

His pulse galloped out of control. "Why? What happened?"

"Stop it, young man. Nothing happened. I'm just glad to see you." She studied him for a moment. "Looks like you could use some comfort food."

"I wouldn't turn it down." He followed Miss Emily through the living room and toward the kitchen. "Where's Jennie?" He glanced down the hall hoping to catch a glimpse of her.

"She ate earlier and went to take a nap." The woman checked her watch. "She should be making an appearance pretty soon."

"Sorry I'm late. We had a call that came in a few minutes before I planned to relieve Officer Hanes during my lunch."

"Don't you worry about a thing, son. Jennie's doing fine. She's a tough cookie, that one." Miss Emily rested her hand on David's shoulder and placed his plate on the table.

"Thank you, ma'am."

"You are so very welcome." Miss Emily lowered herself onto a kitchen chair.

The two sat and chatted, sharing family stories. When he finished his meal, the tension in his muscles had released. Miss Emily had a way of easing a person's stress.

He helped with the dishes and meandered into the living room. He still had thirty minutes.

"Hey there, stranger." A raspy voice entered behind him.

He shifted and gazed at Jennie. Her color had returned, and her eyes were brighter than this morning. She was definitely on the mend. "Hey back. You're looking better."

"I'm feeling better." She joined him on the couch. "You on the other hand look like you lost your teddy bear."

He chuckled. "Leave it to you to notice."

"Well?" She twisted. Tucking her ankle under her knee, she draped her arm on the back of the sofa and winced. "What has my bodyguard all twisted in knots?"

Did he dare ask? He wanted to confirm his beliefs about battered women, but did he dare ask?

"I'm not sure you'll want to hear it." He reached out and tucked a loose strand of hair behind her ear.

She squinted and studied him. "One of two things. Either you rescued or recovered a child this morning, or it has something to do with domestic violence."

His jaw dropped. How did she read him so easily? "How did you know that?"

"Easy." She rubbed the crease in his brow. "Only those two things put that line right here. Everything else, you seem to roll with the punches. Pun not intended."

He ran his hand over his face. "An abused woman screamed at me to let her abusive husband go. Pleaded with us not to arrest him."

"I understand that."

"I don't want to bring up bad memories for you."

"But you want to know why." It was a statement, not a question.

He nodded. "It's just that I'm confused. The women always tell us after things settle down that the husband hadn't meant to hurt them. But I don't get how they can go back to the abuse time and time again." He hoped he hadn't upset her, but he really did want to understand.

She exhaled. "It's not always about that the woman believing her husband or boyfriend won't do it again. It's more about dependence."

He shifted to face her. "Explain."

"He might be her only source of income. If he's in jail, where will she buy food for herself or her children? And then it might come down to being afraid to be alone."

He clasped her hand and squeezed. "Is that the way it was for you?"

"Kinda." She stared at the floor.

David waited. He'd ask her to delve into the darkness of her past, he wouldn't rush her to finish her thoughts.

She shook her head. "For me...it was conditioning."

David tilted his head. What did that mean?

"Everything started in a wonderful way. My husband's friend, helping me out and giving me the support I needed. Then over time, he gaslighted me. I started thinking I was worthless and couldn't fend for myself. By the time he started the physical abuse, I believed I deserved it."

"Please tell me you don't think that anymore." David held his breath. This sweet woman had been through so much.

She laughed. "You seriously have to ask? No. I know that I'm worth more than being a doormat for that egotistical jerk..." She inhaled deeply and released the breath. "I will never be dependent on anyone like that again."

And there it was. The fence erected between them. He didn't want her dependence.

"Jennie, I want your trust. Because, believe me, I'm not all that dependable."

"I do trust you, David. Otherwise, I wouldn't be sitting here. Don't get me wrong. I'm happy you are watching out for Zoey and me, but I have a feeling you're the one keeping secrets now."

And just like that, she zeroed in on the problem. He rubbed the back of his neck, debating whether or not to come clean. What if she turned her back on him? Didn't trust him anymore? "You told me your darkest secret. I suppose it's only fair I tell you mine."

She shook her head. "No. This isn't about fair. It's about you wanting to open up to me."

"I want to. You deserve to know." He held her gaze, determined to tell her how he'd failed the woman he once loved. "Four years ago, I was engaged to a woman named Brenda. I don't know why, but she put up with me. I was different then. Work came first. My relationship with her and my faith were afterthoughts. Something I've changed since then." He swallowed the emotions that crept up his throat. "We had dinner plans. I'd promised her I'd pick her up, but I was running late—like usual. She told me she'd meet me at the restaurant. I agreed since it meant I could finish up what I was working on. Brenda called me a little later saying she had a flat tire. The street she was stuck on wasn't the safest. I knew that, but I told her to hang tight, and I'd be there as soon as I finished up at work."

Jennie cupped his cheek and her thumb wiped under his eye.

He hadn't realized tears trickled down his face. "A half an hour later I received a call from my commanding officer. Brenda had been shot and killed during a mugging. It was my fault she was on that street without help. I ignored her, thinking my work was more important than the woman I loved."

"So that's why you watch out for Zoey and me."

"I can't lose someone else I care about." He placed his hand on top of hers. Their combined hands warmed his cheek.

"You care about me?"

"Jennie. Somewhere along the line, I've fallen for you."

She leaned in and pressed her lips to his.

Without questioning his actions, he deepened the kiss. He hadn't allowed himself to consider a relationship with another woman until Jennie crashed into his life. Reluctantly, he pulled away. "Wow."

Her timidness was adorable. "I shouldn't—"

"Don't you dare apologize," he smiled. "I wish I would have had the strength to kiss you first."

Her face brightened with confidence. "I didn't think I'd ever want to be with another man, but you're making me question that."

"I never thought I could love another woman again, too afraid I'd fail her, but you're making me rethink my stance." He closed his eyes and gathered all the courage he could muster. "Would you be willing to try at a relationship together?"

She bit her lower lip. "Yes, but…"

"What is it?"

"Please don't do anything controlling. I can't handle that."

"I want to be your partner, not demanding."

"Okay."

"As in you'll go out on a date with me and see where this leads?"

She nodded.

He tucked her next to him and rested back on the couch. "For the first time in a long time, I'm looking forward to the future."

She giggled. Actually giggled, and it was the most amazing sound he'd ever heard.

Twenty minutes later, David's phone rang with Zoey's ringtone. He furrowed his brow. "That's Zoey."

Jennie straightened as he answered.

"Zoey?"

"Help." Her voice, barely above a whisper.

"Zoey, what's wrong?" David jerked to his feet and grabbed his keys.

"He's after me."

"Where are you?" He headed for the door.

"I'm in the bathroom at school. I pushed the metal trash can against the door, and I'm hiding in the stall."

"Smart girl. I'm on my way. Don't come out for anyone but me. Got that?"

"Okay."

"Don't hang up. I'm handing the phone to your momma while I call dispatch." He punched the speaker button and handed the phone to Jennie and traded phones with her.

Jennie's fingers shook as she clasped his phone. "Hi, baby."

"Hi, Momma." Sobs sounded from the other end. "I'm scared."

"I know, sweetie. But we're on our way."

David tried to ignore the mother-daughter conversation as he called for assistance.

"9-1-1 what's your emergency?"

"Gloria, it's Whitman. I need units at Roosvelt Elementary code 3."

"Copy that, detective."

"Suspect on site, Zoey Nielson claims someone is after her. She's locked herself in the bathroom."

"Brandon and Hanes are on the way."

"Thanks. Keep me posted. Use Jennie's phone. Zoey's on mine."

"Got it. And detective, keep that little girl safe."

"I'm going to try my best."

He hung up and focused on Zoey and Jennie's conversation.

A clank of metal pierced the air, and a male voice sounded. "Zoey? Come on out. You can't hide forever."

Zoey whimpered.

David sucked in a breath. He was going to be too late. "Stay strong, princess. Help's almost there."

Sirens sounded in the background.

A curse filled the room, and a door slammed shut.

Panic clawed up David's throat. "Zoey?"

Soft sobs filtered over the line. "I'm here. I think he's gone."

***

Jennie followed as David flashed his badge at police officers creating a perimeter around the elementary school and grabbed her hand. They sprinted into the school and hurried down the quiet hall since the students were on lockdown in the classrooms. Her worst nightmare had almost happened if it hadn't been for her daughter's quick thinking, and David giving Zoey his phone number.

When they reached the bathroom, David called out, "Zoey?" He eased inside, weapon drawn.

Tears pricked Jennie's eyes. She held her breath as she waited in the hall. At least she tried. Unable to handle not knowing what was happening, she peered around the corner.

Zoey peeked out from the bathroom stall. "Mr. David?"

"Come here, sweetie." He holstered his gun and held his arms open. Zoey shot from her hiding spot and fell into his embrace. "I think someone else needs a big hug." He released her and shifted her to see Jennie.

Jennie swallowed past the lump in her throat and stepped into the doorway. "Zoey."

Her daughter launched herself into her arms. Jennie staggered. David's hand reached out and steady her. Zoey's arms squeezed around her already sore neck, but Jennie ignored the pain. It was worth it to have her daughter safe in her arms.

"Let's head out and see what Brandon and Randy found out." David spoke softly into her ear.

She nodded, unable to speak past the emotions clogging her throat.

David escorted her and Zoey to the front office and offered her a seat.

She lowered onto the cushioned chair. Zoey curled up on her lap. At least as much as a ten-year-old could.

David squatted beside them. "Zoey. Did you know the man after you?"

Zoey's face scrunched. "I don't think so. But..."

Jennie brushed the hair from her daughter's face. "It's okay, honey. If you know something, you should let David know."

Zoey's blue eyes met hers. Fear flickered in them.

"Go ahead, tell him."

Zoey sighed. "I didn't recognize him, but there was something familiar about him."

David tilted his head. "As in you've seen him around school before?"

"No. I don't think so." Zoey's little fingers traced the hand marks on Jennie's neck. "Like in a picture or something."

"David, could Kenny be responsible for this?" Her heart hammered against her ribcage.

Her daughter shook her head. "It wasn't him."

"Do you know what he looks like?" David asked.

"She's seen pictures of him. I made sure of it." Jennie had struggled with that decision, but in the long run, she wanted her daughter to have the information for her own safety.

"So, not Kenny." David scratched the growing scruff on his jaw.

Brandon rushed in. "Do you need the ambulance?"

David's gaze never left her as he responded to his partner. "No. Zoey's scared but not hurt."

Brandon cleared his throat and stepped closer. "I got a call right before dispatch sent us here."

Jennie's face heated. "And?" She demanded.

Brandon's gaze darted between her and David. "Kenny didn't do this. He hasn't violated his parole. He's with his new girlfriend at a resort in Indiana. Confirmed by security footage."

"Then who is tormenting us?" Jennie rested her cheek on Zoey's head and let the tears fall. The only thing she knew for sure was that she had to keep Zoey safe, no matter what happened to her.

***

David collapsed on the recliner in Jennie's living room. He closed his eyes and thanked God for protecting Zoey. The cloud of failure of figuring out who targeted Jennie and her daughter hung over his head, but he refused to allow it to consume him. He'd spent the last four hours reassuring the mother daughter duo that he and Brandon wouldn't stop until they arrested whoever had turned their life upside down.

Jennie stirred on the couch. She tucked Zoey tighter against her and relaxed, falling back to sleep.

The pair had wormed their way into his heart. He'd do anything to protect them.

The front door opened. He popped to his feet and reached for his Glock. Brandon waltzed in. David's shoulders sagged in relief. He held a finger to his lips and whispered, "Shh. They finally fell asleep twenty minutes ago." He motioned for his partner to join him in the kitchen.

"Here's what you asked for." Brandon handed him the item and dropped onto a seat. "How are they doing?"

David pocketed the rubber bracelet. "Worried. Exhausted." He pulled a chair near Brandon and collapsed onto it. "I'm at a loss. We know Eddie isn't after them, and Kenny's out of the equation, assuming he didn't hire someone, but that doesn't seem likely. We have nothing to go on."

His partner drilled him with a stare.

"What?"

"There's a reason I came over."

David lifted a brow and motioned for him to continue.

"The police department where Tina lives called the station a little while ago. Tina came home from her work trip to a break-in. Someone destroyed her home, looking for something specific."

"And?"

"Once they allowed her into the house, she had a bad feeling about the motive and immediately went to her safe."

"Would you please get to the point?"

"It was open." Brandon wiped a hand down his face. "That's where Tina stored Jennie's address and any pictures they share."

David closed his eyes and took a shuddering breath. "Whoever broke in is after Jennie. And knows where she lives."

Brandon nodded. "The officers said, according to the evidence, the break-in occurred the day Tina came to visit Jennie."

The new information swirled in his mind. David rose and strode over and placed his hands on the kitchen counter and lowered his head. "Who would do that?" Sweat popped out on his forehead and swallowed the bile creeping up his throat. "It's someone from Jennie's past. Only a friend or acquaintance from her time in Indiana would know she'd confide in Tina."

"We need to wake Jennie and get a list of people she knew from back then. But, David, there's another problem."

He swung around to face his partner. "What?"

"The emergency key ring Tina kept in the safe is missing."

"Don't tell me." David stomach twisted into a knot.

Brandon exhaled. "Jennie's house key was on the ring."

"What about my key?" Jennie's question had both men freezing in place.

***

Jennie had tucked Zoey in on the couch and went searching for David. She hadn't expected to discover him and Brandon talking about her house key. The headache that she'd woken up to and the stress of the day had taken a toll. Her patience was running low right now.

She shoved her fists on her hips and glared at the men in her kitchen. "Well? Are you going to stand there or are you going to tell me what's going on."

"I...uh..." Brandon shoulders drooped. "I got a call from the PD where Tina lives. Someone broke into her house."

"And?"

"They found your address."

"They have my house key, don't they?" Jennie wrapped her arms around her waist. The person who had come close to taking Zoey had access to her home. Her eyes drifted toward her bedroom. Had the man been in here?

David moved in front of her. "Jennie? What are you thinking?"

"The other night, when we were on the phone, I felt like someone was watching me."

"I remember." He stiffened. "Brandon."

"I'm on it." Brandon strode from the room.

"What's he doing?"

David's gaze landed on the floor. He rubbed the back of his neck.

"Tell me. Don't keep secrets from me."

"He's checking for cameras in your bedroom."

She gasped. Had her tormentor watched her sleep?

David placed his hands on her shoulders. "We will figure out who is behind all this."

Unable to wrap her mind around all that had happened, Jennie nodded.

A few minutes later, Brandon joined them. He held up the teddy bear Brad had given her years ago in one hand and a small device in the other.

"What's that?"

"This is a camera. Someone hid it in here." He pointed to the stuffed animal's eye.

Tears sprang in her eyes. "And it was pointed at my bed."

Brandon's apologetic look almost took her to her knees. "Yes."

"He's been in my house. Touched my things. Watched me." Her body shook at the revelation.

"Jennie." David's hands moved up and down her arms. "We *will* find him."

Tears streamed down her face. "But will it be too late?"

CHAPTER 17

F riday 8:00 p.m.

David propped himself against the kitchen counter after searching the house for listening devices and hidden cameras and sipped on the caffeine-infused drink that Jennie had made. The coffee—a much-needed boost. He and Brandon had work to do and wouldn't be sleeping in the near future.

"Who would know or suspect that Tina had your information?" He fought the urge to go to her. They required answers to questions to find the person. If he gave into his craving to comfort her, they'd lose precious time.

Jennie rested her elbows on the table and rubbed her temples. "Kenny, of course." She dropped her hands. "According to Tina, Levi and Adam both asked about me. Attempted to pry into my life. Tina didn't budge. She refused to tell them."

"But in the process, her silence most likely confirmed that she knew." Brandon leaned back in his chair and folded his arms.

"It's possible."

"What can you tell us about these two men?" David moved to the table and sat.

"Levi shielded me from Brad on his drunken nights. He'd bring Brad home and put him to bed. Then sit and talk with me."

"Did Brad hurt you during drinking binges?" David wasn't sure he wanted to know but asked anyway.

"No. Never. I think Levi didn't want me to see Brad at his worst." Jennie lifted a shoulder. She traced the rim of her coffee mug with her finger. "Adam was quieter. He'd go drinking with Brad and Levi, but unlike Levi he seemed angry at Brad afterward."

"And after Brad died?" Brandon asked.

"Levi was around a lot, hanging out with Kenny. Adam, not as much, but when he did come over, he paid attention to me and helped with Zoey."

Those two just jumped to the top of David's suspect list. "Anyone else?"

Her mouth twisted to the side. "Tina told me a while back that according to Levi, Kenny's new girlfriend hated me."

David met Brandon's gaze and gestured to the door.

"I'm on it." Brandon stood and strode from the room.

He wrapped Jennie's cold fingers in his hand. "We think you and Zoey should go to a safe house until we can locate the person responsible."

She looked at him like he'd lost his mind. "As if PSPD has the funds for that."

"You're right. We don't have the funds. But I talked with the captain a little while ago. He agrees you need to lie low until we put the pieces together. Brandon's sister has a secluded cabin by the lake she said we could use. And the guys at the station volunteered to stand watch on their off hours."

Her eyes softened. "You all would do that for us?"

"Of course. Why wouldn't we?" He brought her hand to his lips and kissed it. "Please. If nothing else, do this for me. I want you safe."

She seemed torn with what to do. "I don't like asking for help."

"Tell me something I don't know," he muttered.

"Excuse me?" Jennie raised a brow.

"Nothing. So, are you willing to let us protect you?"

She pinched the bridge of her nose. "I suppose. How would this work?"

He exhaled. "We'd sneak you out of the house and drive you to the cabin. We'll park a cruiser in the driveway so people will think we're still watching your house."

"What about Aunt Emily? I don't want her in danger."

"We'll have random patrols go by the house. I don't think whoever this is wants anything to do with her. I promise we'll keep an eye on her."

She peered at him. "When would all this happen?"

"The sooner the better. I'm guessing this guy is out there regrouping after we stopped him. So, we should have a little bit of breathing room, but not much."

"I should go pack a few things then."

He nodded.

Jennie left the kitchen. A few moments later, Zoey stumbled in, sleepy from her nap.

"Hey, Zoey."

The young girl padded over, crawled into his lap, and rested her head on his shoulder. His heart melted.

"I heard you talking."

"You did?"

"Yeah. We're going to a safe house?"

"Are you okay with that?"

"Yes. But I'm scared. What if that man tries to get me again?"

He moved Zoey to one leg and retrieved the rubber bracelet from his pocket. He'd intended to discuss the tracker with Jennie first, but with Zoey's fear of being taken, he'd tell Jennie later. "I have something for you to ensure that doesn't happen." He handed her the wristband.

"What's this?" She took it and slipped it over her hand.

"That's special made just for you. It has a tracker in it. As long as you wear it, I can find you."

"Anywhere?" Zoey's hopeful tone sent daggers into his heart.

"Unfortunately, not anywhere. But within several miles."

Zoey stretched up and kissed him on the cheek. "Thank you."

His heart exploded into pieces at the love and trust she put into him. "Why don't you go help your momma pack your things."

"Okay." Zoey jumped down and skipped to the kitchen archway only to turn around. "I'm so happy you're my friend." She hurried off.

"Me too, little girl. Me too." There was no denying it. Jennie and Zoey had stolen his heart. Now, if he could be the man they needed and not fail them.

Not long after Zoey joined her mom, Jennie came back into the living room. "I'm ready."

She plopped two duffel bags and two backpacks by the front door.

"That was fast." She'd shocked David at the speed of her prepping.

"I learned long ago to be efficient."

"Let me call Brandon and tell him we're ready." David dialed his partner and made plans for the transfer.

Twenty minutes later, three vehicles sat in the driveway along with a police cruiser parked on the street. Brandon had joined him in the kitchen while Randy loaded the car.

"Are you ladies ready?" he asked.

Zoey clutched her teddy bear and nodded.

David jerked to a halt at the sight of Zoey. She'd always carried herself with age beyond her years. But today, she looked like a child.

Jennie hitched her purse on her shoulder and lifted her gaze to his. "I think we're good to go."

He blinked away the realization about Zoey and focused on Jennie. "Here's the deal. We'll leave out the back. Stay sandwiched between Randy and me as we head to the gray sedan next to the garage. You and Zoey will get in the back and hunch down in the seat. Once we're away and I'm sure no one is following us, you can sit up. Brandon will take the other car. While Randy stays at your house making it look like he's guarding you."

Randy came bounding up the back steps from taking the bags to the car. "Let's roll."

Jennie took a deep breath. "Come on, Zoey."

They hurried to the car and slipped into the backseat while David moved to the driver's door. He glanced around to see if anyone was watching. He raised his voice to Randy. "Thanks for staying with the ladies, man. I'll be back later after I finish the paperwork."

"Not a problem. I'll take care of them."

David held his breath hoping if there were ears, the ruse would work. *Please let this work.*

He scanned the streets as he drove. No one was visible, but that didn't mean Jennie and Zoey's attacker wasn't out there.

He drove to the station and pulled into the parking lot. He headed for the employee-only section and took a left into the impound lot and drove out the rear exit.

Still, no one had followed. "Okay, I think you can sit up now."

"Are you sure?" Jennie's voice quivered.

If he could only give her assurance that nothing would happen to either one of them. But he'd been there, done that before and it had turned out tragically.

"I haven't seen anyone since we left your house." He glanced in the rearview mirror.

Jennie helped Zoey into her seat and fastened her seatbelt.

Ever since the incident at school, the girl had been quieter than normal.

He glanced in the rearview mirror and found her sound asleep. His eyes widened as he spotted Jennie climbing over the seat and into the passenger's seat.

"You do know that I could give you a ticket for that."

She rolled her eyes. "Oh, please."

"You're safer in the back." His tone was a bit harsher than he intended. But the woman had triggered his protective streak.

She folded her arms across her chest and glared at him.

"What?" Yup, he'd goofed, but he wasn't wrong about her safety.

"I don't like being told what to do. So far I've gone with your lead, but please don't be demanding or keep secrets from me. It leads to dependence and that's something I can't do again. You have to understand that."

"That wasn't my intention. I'm sorry. I should have asked or said it differently." He'd try not to make that mistake again. "But depending on someone to be there for you and dependence because you aren't capable are two different things."

"I'm the one who's sorry. I'm on edge and that makes me a bit touchy." She shifted in her seat and gazed out the window. Several minutes later, she asked, "Will you be there for me?"

He clasped her hand and threaded his fingers through hers. "You know I will. You can count on me." His breath hitched. Hadn't he said the exact same thing in the past? The times when tragedy had struck. He vowed to himself that things would be different this time.

His phone rang. He released Jennie's hand and hit the hands-free button. "Whitman."

"You have a tail." Brandon didn't waste time getting to the point.

"What? When?"

"Dark blue pickup truck three cars back. He picked you up about five minutes ago."

"How did he know?"

"Unclear, but watch yourself."

"Where are you?"

"I'm about four cars behind him. I'll try to move up and cut him off."

"Roger that." He gripped the steering wheel tighter, turning his knuckles white. "I don't understand. How did he figure it out?"

Jennie clasped her hands together in her lap and glanced in the backseat where Zoey lay sleeping.

"What now, David?"

"We continue weaving through side streets and pray Brandon occupies him long enough for us to get to the cabin without being seen."

Tears streamed down Jennie's cheeks. "Why won't he leave us alone?"

"I've been wondering the same thing. I think he has a god complex. He thinks that he owns you and anything that's yours."

"That sounds like Kenny."

The squeal of tires and Brandon's voice broke through. "He spotted me. Jerk cut the cars in front of me off. Almost caused an accident. Be careful, Whitman. It'll take me a few minutes to get away from this mess. I've alerted Hanes. He's on his way."

"Copy that." David hung up and scanned his rearview mirror.

The blur of blue sent his pulse racing. "Hold on, Jennie, he's coming up fast."

She whimpered and grabbed the edge of her seat.

The truck bumped the rear of his sedan.

He fought to maintain control.

The truck pulled into the left lane and sped up.

Having nowhere to go but forward, David hit the gas and lurched forward.

"Where's my backup?" He needed his partner, now.

The blue pickup raced forward and slammed into the front quarter panel of the vehicle. David's car careened off the road and the passenger's side slammed against a tree. The sickening crunch of metal turned David's stomach. Airbags exploded and silence descended.

A smack on the hood and muted cursing wafted in the air.

The creak of the back door registered in David's brain.

"I'll be back, you good for nothing piece of trash." The man growled.

David struggled with his seatbelt. He watched in the side mirror as a man carried Zoey away, dumped her in his truck, and sped off.

Warm liquid trickled over his eyelid and down his face. He swiped at the offending substance and instantly regretted it. He sucked in a breath and the world spun around him. He shifted his gaze to his right.

Jennie's head rested against the cracked window. Her eyes were closed.

David reached for her wrist. Her steady pulse released the knot in his stomach. He attempted to grab his phone, but hot, searing pain shot up his side. His stomach roiled with each movement.

"Whitman!"

He turned his head.

Brandon came skidding to a stop next to his door. "Dude, you look awful."

"Thanks, man. Jennie needs help."

"So do you. Ambulance is on the way."

There was something he had to tell his partner, but a fog inhabited his brain. David closed his eyes. *Think.* His heart rate increased. "Zoey. He has Zoey."

Brandon peered in the backseat and grabbed his cell. "Dispatch. I need an Amber Alert on Zoey Nielson. Last seen with a male in a navy-blue truck." He rattled off a partial plate number then hung up. He peered into David's window. "Looks like you're stuck pretty good."

When had he rolled down the window?

His partner brushed pieces of glass from the opening.

He blinked. The window wasn't down, it had shattered.

"Hold on, partner."

David watched Brandon fight with the door.

Grunts and creaks filled the silence. The door opened and hung at an awkward angle.

Brandon leaned over David. "Here." His partner cut away the seatbelt and helped David out of the vehicle.

David's disjointed thoughts started to coalesce.

Sitting a few feet away, David could only observe as his partner made his way to Jennie's door.

"No go, partner. Her door is blocked by the tree. Might have been why the dude didn't take Jennie. He had to settle for her daughter instead."

David rested his forearms on his knees and dropped his chin to his chest.

He'd allowed a deranged man to kidnapped Zoey. Jennie would never trust him. He'd obviously failed—again.

***

An hour later, Jennie sat in a conference room at the hospital waiting for David to be released. The man had a mild concussion and stitches on his forehead. But his real injury was the blow he'd taken to his side.

The truck had rammed into the driver's side door, slamming it against him.

She'd heard them discuss internal injuries as they'd whisked her away.

Brandon had stayed by her side and found an empty conference room. The sweet man had even brought in a recliner for her.

She rested her head against the seat. Her heart twisted. Where was her little girl? She could only pray whoever had Zoey didn't hurt her. She thought she'd escaped a man's possessiveness. Escaped abuse. And here she was again, fearing not only for her life, but Zoey's too.

She closed her eyes. "I will find you, sweetheart. Even if it's the last thing I ever do."

"Jennie?"

Warmth on her arm and a low timbre roused her. Her eyes fluttered open. A haze covered her vision. "David?"

"Sorry. It's Brandon."

She pushed herself to a seated position and rubbed her eyes. "I can't believe I dozed off."

"I can. Your body's taken a serious beating lately. Not to mention the car accident."

"How's David?"

"Driving the doctors crazy."

She released a long steady breath.

Brandon pulled up a chair next to hers. "He'll be sore but fine. How are you doing?"

"Wanting my baby back."

"I get it."

Jennie knew the man understood. With two teenagers of his own, he'd understand the panic she felt. "Any news?"

"Not yet. Hanes and the others are on it. I didn't want to leave you alone and besides, the doctors needed protection from my partner." He chuckled.

She forced a smile. "When will David be released?"

"A few minutes ago," A familiar baritone rang from the doorway.

She pushed herself from the recliner and rushed to him. Her gaze traveled his body as she tried to figure out how to hug him without hurting him.

As if reading her mind, he placed his arms around her.

She rested her cheek on his chest. "I'm so glad you're okay."

"I was worried about you. The doctors wouldn't tell me anything." He kissed the top of her head.

"Zoey's missing."

"I know, honey. We'll find her."

Brandon cleared his throat. "If you two are done, my car is downstairs. Let's get to the cabin and discuss our plan to get your daughter back."

She sat next to David in the backseat on the quiet drive and stared out the window lost in thought. David appeared to be consumed with his own thoughts as the miles flew by.

Thirty minutes later, after so many twists and turns that Jennie had no idea where they were, Brandon pulled off the road and down a private drive. At the end of the path stood a cottage. Lights illuminated the front porch. The rocking chairs gave it a perfect getaway vibe. Only it wasn't a peaceful retreat, it was her hiding spot.

She clenched her jaw. How could she sit here knowing her daughter was out there in the presence of pure evil?

She stepped from the car. Her muscles cramped, and she grimaced as she walked a few steps trying to unknot them. She peered over the top of the car.

David grabbed the top of the door and hung his head.

The poor man had to be hurting.

"You okay over there?" She walked around the vehicle.

His shoulders rose and fell. "Yeah, just give me a minute."

She wrapped her arm around his waist and helped him up the three steps to the entrance.

Brandon held the door open and took David's weight as the two of them escorted him to the couch.

"Why don't you and David take a break? I'll go start some coffee." Brandon removed his windbreaker and tossed it over the recliner.

"Sounds like a good idea." She shifted and looked at David. "You should really still be in the hospital."

"Nothing they can do. I'd just be lying around. Here, I can at least help." He twisted to face her and winced.

"Okay, kids. Coffee's brewing. Let's put our heads together and figure this out while we wait." Brandon lowered himself onto the easy chair and crossed his ankle over his knee. "Randy will be here in about five minutes with all the files and a couple more laptops."

"Thanks, man. Appreciate it." David tilted his head back and closed his eyes.

She exchanged glances with Brandon, and he shrugged.

Her nerves felt like live wires. She had to do something besides sit here. She pushed from the couch and paced. Her steps, an experience in pain, but she had to move.

"How did he find us?" Jennie's voice squeaked.

David opened one eye. "The question of the century."

CHAPTER 18

D avid's head swam. If only the throbbing headache would go away so he could think straight His body screamed at him to relax, but with Zoey missing, how could he? He'd messed up. He prayed his mistake didn't cost the young girl her life.

"Who is doing this?" Brandon leaned forward, elbows on his knees and fingers steepled under his chin.

"I honestly don't know." It pained him to know he'd failed Zoey and Jennie.

"It's my fault. I was the one who made bad choices and put her in danger." Tears trickled down Jennie's cheeks.

A knock on the door had all three of them shifting their attention to the entry.

"That should be Randy. It's time to put the pity parties away and focus on finding Zoey." Brandon rose and answered the door.

Officer Hanes strode in, his arms loaded with files and laptops. "Hey y'all. Where do you want this stuff?"

"On the table's fine." David stood and the room spun. He grabbed the back of the couch and steadied himself.

Jennie clutched his arm. "You sure you should be up and working?"

"I can rest after we find Zoey." He'd lost his heart to that little girl the moment she'd called him about the texting mix-up. He made his way to the table. "What do we have?"

"Rick and Sandy from your team will be here soon." Hanes spread the information out and booted up two laptops. "Mags is running down the information you asked for on Levi, Adam, and Kenny's girlfriend. She said she's throwing in a profile on Kenny as well."

"Good. Hopefully, she'll have it soon. And as for Rick and Sandy, we need all the brain power we can get." Brandon sat and gestured to the empty chair. "Sit down before you fall down."

David obliged. He prayed he'd last long enough to point in a direction to investigate.

"I know we put out an Amber Alert, but I want to make sure we didn't miss anything. The stress level was high, and we might have missed a detail." Brandon grabbed a pen and paper. "Go over the events one more time."

David and Jennie took turns filling the two officers in on the details.

"Nothing new there." Brandon tapped his pen.

Officer Hanes looked up from the computer screen. "What was Zoey wearing?"

"Jeans and a purple sweatshirt." Jennie added.

Hanes typed without looking at the keyboard. "What about under the sweatshirt?"

Jennie shook her head. Her voice rose to panic levels. "I don't remember."

David stared at the vase in the middle of the table. "It was a light blue t-shirt with paw prints on it."

Jennie gasped. "Yes, that's it."

David straightened and wince at the pain shooting down his side. Why hadn't he remembered earlier? "She's wearing a dark purple rubber bracelet that I gave her before we left the house."

"The one you had me put the tracker in?" Brandon asked.

"You gave her a tracker?" Hurt filled Jennie's eyes.

"Yes. Before we left your house." David cringed as he remembered Jennie's words about secrets. "I'm sorry. I told Zoey, and I promise I planned on telling you as well, but things moved fast after that."

Jennie stiffened. "Fine. Then find her and arrest the guy responsible for taking her so we can go home."

A woman saying 'fine' was never a good thing. And in this case, he'd royally messed up. His intent was good, but with her background... He pulled up the app on his phone and checked Zoey's location. He came up empty. "It's not that easy, Jennie. We have to be within five miles of her. And according to my phone, she's not within the radius."

"Then what good is your spying on my daughter?" Her voice rose with each word.

"David was only trying to help." Brandon stood up for him.

"I get that. And I'm grateful we might have a way to find Zoey." She spun and leveled him with a glare. "But you had no right to stalk her."

David lowered his head. He'd thought he'd found the woman of his dreams only for his actions to turn it into a nightmare. "We'll find her and bring her home to you."

She raised an eyebrow then faced Brandon, ignoring him. "I need a moment to calm down. If you need me, I'm going to find a bedroom." Jennie disappeared down the hall.

The click of the keyboards and the whoosh of air through the air conditioning vents filled the otherwise quiet space.

Brandon broke the silence. "She'll come around."

David placed a hand on his aching side. "I don't think so." His heart shattered. Zoey was missing, and Jennie...he'd let her down in a big way.

He gritted his teeth and lowered himself onto his seat. All his aches and pains were punishment for not protecting this woman and her daughter.

"Mags emailed the info on our suspects. She's continuing to dig, but she has the preliminary report."

The door opened. Rick and Sandy greeted everyone and joined them at the table.

"Thanks for coming."

"Of course." "No problem." The pair spoke over each other.

"Now that we're all here, tell us what Mags said about Kenny and his friends."

Brandon concentrated on his laptop. "We are all aware of how Kenny ended up in prison. Apparently, he learned his abusive ways from his father. His parole officer has accounted for his whereabouts over the past week."

Rick waltzed in from the kitchen with a cup of coffee and a water bottle. After handing David the mug of bold brew, Rick plopped onto a chair. "He's still on my list. He could have paid off his P.O. to alibi for him."

"True. The man has the biggest motive to terrorize Jennie." David hadn't wanted to consider that option, but it made sense.

"All right, door number two. Levi Benson. Typical bad boy. In trouble as a teen, but nothing major. Oh wait, it says here that fifteen years ago he was arrested for assault. He hauled off and punched a man at a bar for talking to his girlfriend. Nice guy." Brandon rolled his eyes. "Nothing since then though."

Sandy propped her elbow on the table and rested her chin in her hand. "Seems like the jealous type. He could have fixated on Jennie after her husband died."

"Two names, two suspects. I was hoping to narrow things down." David rubbed his eyes. "What about Adam?"

Brandon drummed his fingers on the table. "Adam King had a normal family life growing up. From what Mags discovered, he was a quiet kid and a loner. The only odd thing is a sealed juvenile record. Could be anything. We'd need a warrant to open it."

"That won't happen unless we have evidence to justify it." David eased back in his chair. The bruises from the accident screamed at him. "Jennie said he was quiet, but he helped her with Zoey when he came to visit Kenny. Sounds like the only one out of the three men that seemed to care about Jennie."

"Let's look at motive for a minute." Sandy had them switching gears

Brandon crossed his arms over his chest. "Whoever is responsible is obsessed with Jennie."

"That makes the most sense. Which leads us back to Kenny, who has an alibi." Frustration set in. David wanted to throw his coffee mug across the room.

"True. But whether it's him or one of the others, why take Zoey?" Rick asked.

Sandy stared at the ceiling, her eyes darted back and forth, seeking an answer. "To get back at Jennie. She'd do anything for that little girl."

"I get that. But there has to be more to it." David's brain refused to function. If they didn't figure out who had Zoey soon, he'd be a puddle of sludge on the floor, unable to contribute to the discussion.

Brandon's gaze drifted from one person to the next. "If you ask me, this guy thinks Jennie is his property and anything that belongs to her is his too."

Hanes flipped open a file he'd tossed aside earlier and typed frantically on the computer.

What had triggered Randy's sudden interest?

"Whatcha got?" Rick asked.

Randy held up a finger then went back to typing.

David's heart rate increased at the possibility that Randy was on to something.

***

Jennie sat on the bed. Her face in her hands. Hiccupping sobs shook her body. How had she let herself get into this mess? She'd been desperate for love, that's how. But Aunt Emily had taught her better than to jump at the first man to show her attention. Not that most men were abusive like Kenny, but still. If she'd come home to her aunt, things would have turned out differently for her and Zoey.

"Oh, Zoey, where are you?" Jennie pulled her phone from her pocket and found a photo of her daughter. Her bright blue eyes glimmered with mischief.

She inhaled. She'd do anything to get her baby back.

The phone vibrated, startling her.

She glanced at the Caller ID. *Unknown*.

Could it be the person that took Zoey? She punched the button. "Hello?"

"I imagine you want this pretty little girl back," A slimy voice oozed over the line. She tried to place it but couldn't.

"Don't touch her." Bile rose in Jennie's throat.

"Demanding, aren't we?" he hissed. "Time you figure out who you belong to."

"Who are you?"

"I'm disappointed, Jennie. You haven't figured out who I am?"

The voice sounded familiar, but she couldn't place it. "Let Zoey go. It's me you want."

"You're right."

"Tell me what to do?"

"There ya go, that's my girl. Always wanting to please."

Her skin crawled at the memories of Kenny's touch. This man wasn't Kenny. She knew that much, but she'd do what it took to free Zoey.

The sickening sweet voice sounded over the line. "I'll make a trade. You for your daughter."

"You won't hurt her?"

"I guess you'll have to trust me." He cackled.

Not likely. "Where?"

"There's a car at the gas station on Highway 1. Keys are under the seat and the directions are in the glovebox."

"It'll take me a while to get there." She needed to buy time for the police to get there first.

"Don't lie to me! You have thirty minutes to get here. If you don't, I'll kill her."

Jennie whimpered. "Please don't hurt her."

"And no cops. I see a cop and you both die."

"Fine."

"Remember, thirty minutes. No cops." The man hung up.

She found directions to the gas station, then shoved her phone in her pocket. Her gaze drifted to the door. Should she tell David and his buddies about the call? But what if the guy on the phone found out. He'd kill Zoey. No. She couldn't take that chance. She was on her own again. She slid the window open and slipped outside.

The cool coastal air slammed into her, stealing her breath. Her mind screamed to tell David, but her heart told her to keep moving. She only had thirty minutes.

Using the flashlight app on her phone so she didn't trip, she raced around the corner of the house and jogged along the edge of the road. Her body protested, but she couldn't stop. Tears stung her eyes at the ache flowing through her limbs. She endured so much since all this had started, but she'd put aside the pain to save her daughter.

David's face swam in her thoughts. The man had been there for her every step of the way. She'd overreacted about the tracker, she knew that deep down, but the betrayal lingered. Learning to trust was the lesson she'd yet to master. But if she allowed herself to trust anyone, it would be David.

Ten minutes later, the neon lights of the gas station glowed ahead. Her side ached and her muscles burned.

She slipped to the rear of the building and spotted a lone car. She tried the door, and it clicked open. Reaching under the front seat, she snagged the keys and stood. She lowered her battered body into the driver's seat and leaned across the console to retrieve the address.

She stared in amazement. Zoey was only ten miles from here.

Turning the ignition, she pulled out of the parking lot and aimed the car toward her daughter and her worst nightmare.

Minutes later, she turned onto a dirt path. The trees lining the road blocked the moonlight, casting an intense darkness over the long driveway. A cabin loomed ahead, tucked into the middle of nowhere. She had to trust David if she had any hope of surviving. But how would he ever find her? She'd left without a word, another decision she'd regret for as long as she lived. Which, under the circumstances, might not be long. Jennie owed him an apology for overreacting.

She glanced at her phone. The screen toggled between no service and one bar. She shared her location then typed in a text message and hit send, praying the message would go through.

Leaving the phone on, she placed it in the console hoping the guys found her by using the GPS.

She rushed up the path to the rustic cabin ahead. Her footfalls crunched in the dry grass and leaves. Had the man already hurt Zoey? Did he have any intension of letting her daughter go?

God, please let my text go through.

"Ahhh, baby. Good to see you again." Adam stood on the front porch, arms crossed with a sickening grin on his face.

The look on his face turned her blood cold. She straightened, determined not to show fear. "I'm here. Let Zoey go."

"Not so fast, sweetheart. Come on in." He turned and disappeared through the door.

She swallowed. All the times he'd come over and helped with Zoey, she should have realized he wasn't as kind as he appeared. He had to have been aware of Kenny's abuse and had done nothing to save her.

Could she step into the unknown?

She had to. Her daughter's life was at stake.

She moved through the doorway. Her gaze landed on Zoey tied to a chair in the small living room.

Her daughter's blue eyes flickered with fear.

"It's going to be okay, honey. I'm here. Adam will let you go now."

"Yeah, about that." He stepped closer. His hot, rancid breath brushed her face. "She stays."

Jennie's jaw dropped. "You said…"

Without warning, he slapped her.

She cupped the stinging flesh.

"Time for you to realize who owns you. And whatever is yours is mine." Adam chuckled.

Terror tore through her. She'd moved away from Indiana without a word to protect Zoey and herself. No notification to Brad's friends or the police. No forwarding address. All for Zoey's safety—and her own. And now her past had found her.

Adam grabbed her arm and yanked her toward him. "Time for a lesson."

His fists found every injury on her and then some.

Jennie's body had taken a lot of punishment over the past few days, and she didn't have much left in her survival tank.

He threw her backward. Her spine hit the edge of the table, and she slumped forward, dropping to her knees. How had she missed Adam's obsession with her?

She gritted her teeth and lifted her gaze, connecting with Zoey's horrified look.

"Momma?"

"It's okay, honey."

Adam held a knife to Zoey's throat. "Now, make me a sandwich like a good little woman, or the brat is dead."

Jolts of pain zapped her body, but she moved to the kitchen and prepared a plate for him. Anything at this point to give her and Zoey time. While she spread mayo on the bread, she prayed David had received her text and was on the way.

She placed the meal on the table. "Here."

Adam grabbed a chair and slammed the feet on the floor next to Zoey. "Sit." He jerked her arm.

She bit back a cry and stumbled onto the chair.

"Don't move." His evil laugh sent chills racing down her spine. He swaggered to the table, flipped on the radio, and sat with his back to them. He sang to the song between bites in his off-key tone.

"Momma," Zoey whispered.

"Shh." Jennie shifted her gaze to Adam. The man ate his sandwich like beating a woman was just another day at the office. She returned her gaze to her daughter. "Stay strong. Don't let him see you as weak," she mouthed.

Zoey nodded, tears spilling down her cheeks.

Jennie scanned the room. The living room was connected to the kitchen that included a four-person table, and a small hallway presumably led to the bedroom and bathroom.

She sucked in a breath. White lights danced in her eyes and pain shot through her core. She took in small sips of air. *Don't do that again.*

"Zoey, look at me," she whispered.

Her daughter's eyes met hers.

"If I give you an opportunity to escape, take it."

"No. I'm not leaving you. He'll kill you."

Jennie knew that Zoey was probably right, but she had to get her daughter away from this man. Her daughter still wore the bracelet that David gave her. If the text hadn't gone through, Zoey was the only hope of getting help.

"You're our only hope of getting out of here. When the time comes, run. There's a car parked at the end of this lane. My cell is in the console. Take it. Find service and call David—promise me."

Zoey glanced in Adam's direction then back at her and mouthed *promise.*

Now to figure out how to free Zoey. Adam hadn't tied her to the chair. Most likely he figured she hurt too much to move, and he wasn't wrong. But she had to find a way to untie Zoey and get her out of the cabin.

Jennie lowered her head, pretending she was in too much agony to move. If only it wasn't the truth.

As she sat waiting for the opportunity to free Zoey, she forced herself to relax. She focused on a spot on the floor and prayed that David found them before it was too late.

"Momma," Zoey whispered.

Not enough energy to respond, she raised her eyes.

"He's in the bathroom."

It was now or very literally maybe never. She clenched her teeth and moved toward her daughter. Her swollen limbs made it difficult to move let alone untie the ropes. But if there was ever a time to suck it up and move forward, this was it.

The ropes fell from Zoey's wrists and the girl bolted from her seat. "I'll get help. I promise." Zoey ran straight through the front door and out into the night.

Jennie staggered to her chair and collapsed onto it. Tears trickled down her face. More pain was on the horizon, but at least her daughter was free.

"What did you do?" Adam stormed into the living room. "Why you little..." His fist landed hard across her cheekbone.

She fell to the floor and curled into a ball protecting herself.

Adam continued his abuse.

Her body went numb and darkness pulled her under. Glorious oblivion.

Chapter 19

Saturday 4:00 a.m.

David had made a colossal mistake. Not giving Zoey the bracelet, he'd never feel bad about that. But not asking Jennie's permission or at least informing her right away, for that he'd forever kick himself. Jennie had disappeared into the bedroom well over an hour ago. Time to grovel and hope that one day she'd forgive him.

The prescription dose of ibuprofen had kicked in. He'd take the dull aches over the intense pain any day. He hobbled down the hall to the bedroom. "Jennie?"

When she didn't answer he called out again. "Jennie, are you okay?" He rested his forehead on the door. "Look, I'm sorry. I should have told you. I know that. Please, let me in."

A shiver wove up his spine. "Jennie?" He tested the knob. It turned. He pushed the door open and halted. "Brandon, get in here!" he called over his shoulder.

The room sat empty. The comforter on the bed was slightly rumpled and the lamp on the side table was on. But it was the open window that made his knees buckle.

"Whoa." Brandon caught his elbow before he faceplanted. "What's going—oh." His partner guided him to a chair in the corner of the room.

He dropped onto the seat. "She's gone."

"Good news, it appears she left on her own and not by force."

"But why?" David knew. He'd shattered her trust in him. He stood and strode to the window.

"I see that look. Get out of your head, man." Brandon joined him.

He shook his head. "I shouldn't have gotten personally involved. And we all know I mess things up when it comes to that." He pulled his phone from his pocket and checked the GPS for Zoey's wristband.

"You have got to let go of the past. Yes, you were late meeting with Brenda, but you didn't cause her death. You need to forgive yourself and allow yourself to move on."

He scoffed, "I let Zoey get kidnapped, and Jennie slipped out the window because of what I did."

"Zoey was not your fault. And Jennie is dealing with her own baggage. She'll get over it." Brandon slapped him on the back of the head in a classic Jethro Gibbs move.

David rubbed the spot Brandon smacked. "Ouch. Dude. Car accident. Remember? What was that for?"

"For you being an idiot and wallowing in self-pity. Get out of your head and focus so we can find your girls."

"After the way I let her down? I doubt I'll ever have a chance with Jennie."

Brandon raised his hand and David ducked.

"All right, man. I get the picture. Now quit smacking me."

"As if I hit you that hard." Brandon rolled his eyes.

"David! Brandon!" Rick yelled from the other room.

They rushed to their teammate.

"What's up?" Brandon asked.

"Mags sent the update on our suspects."

David pulled out chairs and sat. "What'd she say?"

"She contacted people she trusted and got eyes on Kenny and Levi. Both are in Indiana, along with Kenny's girlfriend. Adam is unknown. However, she dug deeper into the background of all three. Not a pretty picture, by the way. Mags didn't try to get a warrant for his juvenile records. She did some sleuthing on her own and talked to his father. His mother passed away several years ago from cancer. Adam was rescued from a horrible life and adopted at the age of six. I won't go into details, but needless to say, the things that happened during his formative years were awful. His parents tried to undo all the evil he'd experienced. For the most part they did. But his father said he was obsessive with things he perceived to be his. If they took away something that he attached to, Adam would get violent, even as a child."

"Adam has her. Not Kenny." David let the truth sink in. He spun to Brandon. "We have to get out there and find her now."

The team left Randy to monitor the computers and hurried to the cars. Rick and Sandy went one direction while he and Brandon took off in another.

David scanned the sides of the roads for Jennie or Zoey while Brandon drove along the back roads and county highways.

Five miles, that's all they needed to get a location on Zoey. As for Jennie...he prayed the two were together.

"Anything on that GPS tracker of yours? Which I might add was genius." Brandon continued his visual search as he drove.

"No. Not yet." David's shoulders slumped. He glanced at his phone for the hundredth time. Or so it felt. Still no ping. "Where are you, Jennie?"

"We'll find her."

David couldn't speak. He swallowed the lump in his throat. His phone beeped with an incoming text message.

Jennie: I'm sorry I disappeared. I couldn't take the chance with Zoey's life. I'm praying you find us in time.

"See if you can use her GPS to find where she is." Brandon pulled off on the side of the road. "No sense driving aimlessly."

"I'm on it." David noticed her location share and accepted it. "It's eight miles away."

Brandon called Sandy and Rick, letting them know what they found out, then took off.

David's cell phone rang. Startled, he scrambled to hold on to his phone. "It's Jennie's phone." He pushed the accept button and put the call on speaker. "Hello? Jennie?"

"Help me, please." Sobs filled the airway.

"Zoey?"

"It's me. He's gonna kill Momma if you don't do something quick."

"We're almost there." David glanced at Brandon.

His partner nodded. "Four minutes."

He returned his attention to Zoey. "Honey, are you hurt?"

"I'm okay. He didn't hit me, if that's what you're asking."

He breathed a sigh of relief. Hitting wasn't his only question, but it sounded like the man hadn't laid a hand on her.

"He tied me up."

Zoey's soft voice brought him back to the problem at hand. "What was that?"

"He tied my wrists together behind a chair."

"Oh, honey, I'm so sorry. Hang in there. Can you tell me where you are?"

"Not really. I found the car Momma drove and her cell phone was just where she told me it would be, but I had to walk a little bit to get enough service to call."

"Wait. Your mom was there?"

"Uh huh. She saved me."

"Stay where you are."

"Okay."

A few minutes later, he stepped from the vehicle before Brandon had put it in park.

"Zoey?" he whisper-yelled. "Zoey?"

"I'm right here." Zoey sat under a bush, knees to her chest and tears streaming down her face.

David scooped her up and held her.

Her arms flung around his neck. Hiccupping sobs sounded in his ear.

"I've got you."

She pulled in a deep breath and swiped at her eyes.

"Better?"

She nodded.

He sat her on the backseat of Brandon's car. "Can you tell me what happened?"

Zoey filled him in on how Adam had kidnapped her and tied her to the chair. Then how he'd lured Jennie to them by promising to release Zoey.

"He hit Momma a bunch of times. But when he left the room, she untied me and told me to run." Zoey's eyes shift to the ground. She wouldn't look at him.

"What is it sweetheart? What aren't you telling me?"

Zoey's bottom lip quivered. "She told me to run, but I couldn't just leave her there. So I snuck to the window and peaked in. That's when I saw him hurt Momma really bad. She wasn't moving. I knew I had to run and get you."

David felt the blood drain from his face. He couldn't lose Jennie. And the thought of this man laying a finger on her again, sent anger raging through him.

"Can you tell us where the cabin is?"

Zoey shook her head.

He was so close and yet they had no idea where she was.

"But I can show you."

"What?"

"I didn't take the road, I went through the woods. I can show you."

He hesitated. He didn't want Zoey anywhere near Adam, but to find Jennie, he didn't have a choice.

David nodded. "All right, you can take us, but once we get there you are going with Detective Pratt."

Sandy Pratt stepped up and shook Zoey's hand. "Hi, Zoey."

Zoey accepted the gesture and shifted her gaze to David. "Okay." She paused. "But you'll help my momma, right?"

He knelt next to her. "You know I will." He squeezed her hand. "Give me a second, then you can lead the way."

He stood and walked a few feet away to join Brandon. "Everyone ready?"

"Yup." He handed David a Kevlar vest, sporting the bright yellow word Police. "Rick is ready. He requested an ambulance on stand-by. They'll stay a few miles down the road out of the way once they arrive."

"Then let's get moving." David returned to the car. "You ready, Zoey?"

She slid from the seat. She entwined her fingers with his.

He looked down and the desperate look on her face shattered his heart. "Lead the way."

Zoey plunged into the woods dragging David along with her.

His flashlight illuminated her path. The twigs and bushes crunched under his feet. The poor girl had not had an easy escape.

She stopped and put her finger to her lips. "Shh. See that dirt road?"

He nodded.

"Take that to the right and the cabin is at the end."

He handed Zoey off to Sandy and nodded to his partner and Rick.

Zoey jerked the tail of his jacket. "Be careful. I don't want to lose you too."

A lead ball dropped in the pit of his stomach. He rested his hand on her shoulders. "Don't give up hope."

She swallowed. "Okay."

But he could tell, Zoey had already figured her mother was dead. He just hoped the girl was wrong.

The three of them spread out and marched up to the house.

He peered into the window beside the front door.

Adam nudged Jennie with the toe of his boot. A knife blade glinted in the low light of the cabin. "Come on, woman. Get up." His voice boomed from inside the house.

Jennie struggled to lift her head. Her face, red and swollen. Her eyes, only slits.

David's breath caught. He froze in place. *Jennie.* Her name came out as a whisper.

Anger boiled. He wanted to rip the man limb to limb, but he knew he had to pull it together. Jennie's life depended on him doing his job.

He exhaled and spoke into his mic. "Hostage situation. Everyone in position?"

Affirmatives rang in his ear. He peered into the window once again.

Adam jerked Jennie from the floor and held her around the neck. The blade of the knife rested against her throat.

Lord, please don't let me be too late.

David gave the signal and rushed in, weapon out and aimed at Adam. "Police."

Brandon stood next to him. "Let her go, Adam."

"Why that little brat! Thought she could save her mom, did she?" Spittle flew from his mouth. Adam's arm tightened around Jennie's neck. The silver blade pushed into her skin. Red droplets clung to the steel.

"Don't do it!" David's eyes never left Adam's, but he could see Jennie struggling for air. Her fingers clawing at Adam's forearm. Tears slid down her cheeks.

"Let her go." Brandon's voiced boomed from behind him.

"She's mine. You'll never have her." Adam moved toward the hallway dragging Jennie with him. His eyes darted around the room like a caged animal.

"Come on now, Adam. Jennie was never yours."

Something dark shuttered over Adam's eyes. An evil smile curved on his lips. Then he kissed Jennie's temple.

She grimaced as if the devil himself had touched her.

David gritted his teeth. The desire to put his fist in the man's face was overwhelming. But right now, his priority was Jennie.

"You might as well let her go and put the knife down. There's no way out." David held his aim steady. He watched for a shot, but the blade was too close. One minor flinch and the Adam would slice her throat.

Adam's breathing rate increased. Sweat dripped from his brow.

The man was unstable, and David didn't know how much longer they had before the creep would do something stupid.

"You want this cheating little witch? Then you can have her!" Adam yelled and threw Jennie's limp, semi-conscious body at him and ran down the hall.

David caught her with one arm and cradled her against his chest.

Brandon tore off running after Adam. "I've got him."

David scooped Jennie in his arms and laid her on the couch.

Rick rushed in. "I'll take care of her. Go."

He placed a kiss on her forehead and stared at Rick for a moment, willing his teammate to protect her with his life.

Rick nodded.

With assurance Jennie would be safe, David sprinted through the front door and around the back of the house in time to see Brandon climb through a small window and take off into the woods.

Faint light filtering through the trees. He caught a glimpse of a figure dodging brush and limbs. David's long legs ate up the ground. His injuries hidden by adrenaline. Catching up with Brandon, the two pumped through the dense growth.

"He's headed to the highway." Brandon pointed toward the end of the woods.

Drumming footfalls and labored breaths filled the night air.

Adam sprinted up the small embankment and onto the road.

Tires squealed. David crested the ditch just in time to see Adam's body tumble over the hood of a car and slam onto the ground with a thud.

He jumped over the edge of the road and ran to where Adam lay. He kept his gun aimed at the man until Brandon joined him.

His partner knelt next to the man's body and placed two fingers on his neck. "He's still alive. Better get the ambulance."

David held his position until Brandon finished his search for additional weapons. Although, the action was in vain. Adam wasn't getting up from the accident. In fact, it would be a miracle if he lived.

Holstering his Glock, David grabbed his radio and requested paramedics, adding, "Jennie comes first. Then you can save this sleaze ball."

"Copy that. Ms. Nielson is already in route to the hospital, and Detective Pratt is following with Zoey." a voice from the speaker stated.

Adrenaline fading, David rested his hands on his knees and sucked in air. He tilted his head, finding his partner on one knee with his head in his hands inhaling just as heavily.

Everything in David wanted to race to the hospital and be with Jennie. Wanted to make sure she was okay.

He huffed in frustration. "I don't even know her condition."

Brandon shifted and met his gaze. "She was alive when we found her. Hang on to that."

Praying was all he could do. His job required him to stay and handle the situation at hand.

But what if Jennie didn't make it? How would he ever survive?

***

Jennie's body screamed in pain. Every inch of her hurt. It even hurt to blink. She had no idea where she was. She could still be on the floor of the cabin for all she knew. But she didn't care. Her body throbbed in time with her heartbeat.

"Jennie?" a low husky voice faded in and out.

The voice was soothing, and she loved the sound of it.

"Jennie, honey? Are you there?"

The puzzle pieces floated together. David. Zoey. Adam.

She sucked in a deep breath and cried out in pain.

Gentle hands smoothed back the hair from her forehead.

The touch almost more than she could bear.

"Jennie, I'm right here." David's low timbre cleared her muddled mind.

"Zoey?" The desert in her mouth made her words come out as a croak.

"She's safe."

Something cold pressed against her lips.

"Open your mouth for some ice chips, honey."

She obliged. The relief was incredible.

"Better?"

"Yes," she whispered. Her eyelids lifted, and the most wonderful sight came into focus.

David leaned over the rail of a bed.

"Hospital?"

"Yes." His voice quivered. "You scared me, Jennie."

"Adam?" She felt stupid for the one-word questions, but she didn't have the strength to say more.

"In surgery."

She scrunched her forehead and grimaced. "What happened?"

"You don't need to worry about that right now."

He wanted to protect her, she knew that deep down, but she had to know. She didn't want to be babied. She wanted—needed—to feel in control. At least when it came to Adam.

"Tell me."

David nodded, seeming to understand. "He was hit by a car when he tried to run from us. The doctors aren't sure if he'll make it."

Jennie didn't know whether to rejoice the fact or feel sorrow for the man who'd kidnapped Zoey and hurt her. A tear slid down her temple.

"Honey, what's wrong?"

"I don't know," she whispered. Yet, she did know. Her choices had put Zoey in danger.

"Honey, Adam made his own choices. You didn't do anything to cause that."

"Maybe."

"No maybe about it. He's a sick and twisted man."

She closed her eyes and tried to make sense of Adam's obsession with her.

David's fingers intertwined with hers. "Go to sleep. You're safe. I'm not leaving."

Warmth spread through her. The man she'd fallen in love with was staying right by her side even after the way she'd treated him.

Her limbs felt heavy, and her mind slid toward darkness once again.

CHAPTER 20

Saturday 3:00 p.m.

David had pulled up a chair early in the a.m. when Jennie had fallen asleep and wrapped her hand around his. Jennie's pain levels had been off the charts a couple of times. Her whimpers had broken his heart. Only after she'd settled down and Brandon informed him of Adam's death had David fallen into a deep sleep for a few hours.

The afternoon sun shone through the blinds. Aunt Emily had brought Zoey by to see her mom after they'd moved Jennie from an emergency bay to a regular hospital room. Jennie woke to reassure her daughter for a few minutes before exhaustion pulled her under.

"David?" He tore his gaze from the woman he loved and landed on Brandon.

"Yeah," he whispered.

His partner slipped inside the room. "How's she doing?"

"It's been a rough day, but I think she's finally resting a little easier now."

"Glad to hear it. She's one tough lady."

David shifted his gaze to the battered woman next to him. "I could have lost her."

"Yes, you could have, but you didn't. And if the worst would have happened, it wouldn't have been your fault."

"I don't know about that." He shook his head.

"I do. I'm not sure I could have kept it together out there if it was the woman I loved. You did what you had to do. I am proud to call you my partner."

Loved? Who was he kidding? Jennie and Zoey had become everything to him. "Thanks, man." He lifted his hand and ran his fingers through his hair. Brandon was right. He had put it all aside and did his job. Because if he hadn't, he would have lost everything again.

"So? Are you going to give yourself a break now?"

David scrunched his brow. "What do you mean?"

Brandon rolled his eyes. "Serious-ly? Mr. I-can't-trust-my-own-judgement-when-someone-I care-about-is-involved."

He exhaled. He had trusted his judgement out there, and his decisions had been the right ones. Jennie being alive and breathing next to him was proof. It hit him like a baseball bat across the back of his head. He didn't control life and death. He could only do what he thought was best under the circumstances.

"You're right."

Brandon snickered. "Say that again."

David tried to smother a grin. "I said, 'You're right.'"

"That's what I thought." His partner beamed with mischief.

"I think I like you better when you're wrong." David huffed.

Brandon turned serious. "She's gonna be okay?"

"According to the doctors, yes." He rubbed his thumb along the back of her hand. "At least physically."

"That's a start. You both can work on the emotional once she recovers."

"Assuming she forgives me for not telling her about the wristband."

Jennie's hand tightened on his. "She forgives you."

David gently cupped her cheek, careful of her injuries. "I'm the one who's sorry for overstepping."

She leaned into his touch. "I shouldn't have jumped to conclusions. You were only trying to help."

Brandon cleared his throat, reminding David he and Jennie weren't alone. "I'm going to...um...yeah, I'll check in later." His partner strode out of the room.

He returned his gaze to Jennie. "You really forgive me?"

She smiled, then cringed from the pain. "I do."

David closed his eyes and thanked God he hadn't messed up a future with this woman.

***

Sunday 11:00 a.m.

Sleep had done Jennie a world of good. Her aches and pains had dulled. But maybe that had something to do with the medicine flowing through her IV. More than that, her heart had settled since she and David had apologized to each other and had agreed on a fresh start between them.

"You look like you're feeling better." David sauntered in and took the seat he'd occupied since she'd woken up in her hospital room.

"I am. Still sore and don't plan to move fast, but I'm happy to be alive." The nurse helped raise her bed earlier that morning, making it easier to have a conversation. "Speaking of looking better, you're moving easier."

"A hot shower does wonders." He clasped her hand in his. "Now that we're both a little more coherent, I want to finish our discussion."

"Which one?" She knew exactly what he meant, but she wanted—no, needed—to hear it again.

"I want to date you. Treat you the way you deserve." David exhaled. "I'll mess up again. I can guarantee that. We both have healing that needs to happen, but I want to do it together."

Tears pooled in her eyes. No demands. Only a partnership. "My past will rear its ugly head, but I'm willing to fight for a relationship with you."

A smile graced his handsome face.

"I do have a request."

"And what's that?"

"A kiss to seal the deal."

He stood and leaned in. "I don't want to hurt you."

"You won't. I promise."

His lips tentatively touched hers, gentle, testing at first. He deepened the kiss, making all her dreams come true. A man who respected her. Cared for her and her daughter. All without fear—only love.

EPILOGUE

F our months later

David huddled deeper into his fleece jacket on Jennie's back porch swing with the ocean waves crashing below. The temperatures hovered in the upper fifties, but God had painted a beautiful sunset, and he planned to enjoy it with the love of his life.

The door swung shut behind Jennie, and she handed him a mug of hot chocolate.

"Thank you." He patted the bench beside him. When she sat, he put his arm around her and tugged her closer.

She snuggled into his side and sipped her beverage. "I got a letter from Kenny."

David stiffened. They'd promised not to keep secrets from each other, but he hadn't expected to hear that. He took a deep breath and forced himself to relax. "What did he have to say?"

"I didn't believe the rumors that he wasn't the same man he used to be. But he really has changed. He apologized for what he did and asked for my forgiveness."

"How do you feel about that?"

"I know I'm supposed to forgive him." She scraped her bottom lips with her teeth. "And I do. But is it wrong of me that I never want to see him again?"

He tugged her tighter against his side. "I don't think that's unreasonable."

"Maybe we can talk with our therapist about it next time?"

After she'd physically recovered from her encounter with Adam, they both agreed to see a therapist to work through their respective pasts. A month ago, they decided to see her together. The results had been amazing. "Of course. If that's what you want."

She nodded. "I do."

David nudged the swing into a slow glide. "Adam is gone, and Levi is innocent. From what we can tell, he had no idea what his friend had done. Plus, Kenny's letter gives you closure. It's good to know that he doesn't want revenge but forgiveness. I'm hoping now we can put all that behind us."

"I'd like that." She tipped her head back and smiled.

He'd never take her happiness for granted. "I talked to Zoey."

"Uh-oh, what are you two plotting now?"

"Oh, you think you're funny, don't you?"

"Yes," she giggled. "Sorry. As you were saying."

David set his mug on the ground and cupped her face with both hands. "I want a future with you. You and Zoey. I'm not proposing now, but I want you to know, that's where our relationship is going. If you're not okay with that, please tell me now."

"You're right. I'm not ready—yet. But I can't wait for that time to come."

He pressed his lips to hers and lingered a bit longer than he'd planned. "One more thing."

She tilted her head. Her eyes searched his.

"When we get married, I want to adopt Zoey if that's okay with you and her."

Tears pooled on Jennie's lashes and poured over. She threw her arms around him and kissed him like her life depended on it.

He eased away and rested his forehead on hers. "I'll take that as a yes."

"When you came into my life, you saved me in more ways than one. From Adam and from myself. I'm a different person because of your love. I couldn't ask for a better father for my daughter than you."

David's heart filled with so much love he thought it might explode. He'd lost Brenda and thought he'd wallow in guilt forever. But when he found Jennie, her love brought light to the darkness. He couldn't imagine a future without her and Zoey. And according to Jennie, he wouldn't have to.

Dear Reader Letter

Dear Reader,

Thank you for joining me on this journey.

Shout out to my Suspense Squad girls. Knowing there's a group of writers who I can call at any time for writing help or just to laugh is amazing. Thank you, ladies. And to my writing community, you're awesome.

Let's not forget a special thank you to my law enforcement consultant Detective James Williams, Sacramento Internet Crimes Against Children, who answers all my crazy questions. By the way, all mistakes are my own or are author privileges, so don't complain to him. Lol!

And thank you to my family for their love and support. Love you bunches, Darren, Matthew, and Melissa!

Hugs, Sami

ABOUT Sami A. Abrams

A ward-winning, bestselling author Sami Abrams grew up hating to read. It wasn't until her 30's that she found authors that captured her attention. Now, most evenings, you can find her engrossed in a Romantic Suspense.

She lives in Northern California, but she will always be a Kansas girl at heart. She is a retired teacher and has a love of sports, family, and travel. However, a cabin at Lake Tahoe writing her next story is definitely at the top of her list.

Want more Sami A. Abrams books? Follow her on Amazon:

https://amzn.to/3Y4rnwz

Don't forget to sign up for her newsletter to receive a free short story:

https://bit.ly/3DijJU8

Visit Sami's website for an entire list of her books.

https://samiaabrams.com/

www.ingramcontent.com/pod-product-compliance
Lightning Source LLC
Chambersburg PA
CBHW071556110726
47908CB00007B/2119